Bobcat's Big Adventure

Mark Phillips

"All rights reserved. No part of this book may be reproduced in any form or by any electronic or mechanical means, including information storage and retrieval systems, without written permission from the author, except in the case of a reviewer, who may quote brief passages embodied in critical articles or in a review. Trademarked names appear throughout this book. Rather than use a trademark symbol with every occurrence of a trademarked name, names are used in an editorial fashion, with no intention of infringement of the respective owner's trademark. The information in this book is distributed on an "as is" basis, without warranty. Although every precaution has been taken in the preparation of this work, neither the author nor the publisher shall have any liability to any person or entity with respect to any loss or damage caused or alleged to be caused directly or indirectly by the information contained in this book."

"This is a work of fiction; names, characters, places, and incidents either are the product of the author's imagination or are used fictitiously, and any resemblance to actual persons, living or dead, events, or locales is entirely coincidental."

Contents

Introduction	5
Chapter One – Things Moving Around	7
Chapter Two – In a Box	17
Chapter Three – Jake Jones	25
Chapter Four – Her Dream	35
Chapter Five – First Night Under the Stars	45
Chapter Six – Biff	51
Chapter Seven – Her Dreams Travel West	61
Chapter Eight – Woods and Railway Lines	71
Chapter Nine – Breakfast	79
Chapter Ten – Lucky for One	85
Chapter Eleven – The Playground	93
Chapter Twelve – Two Weeks Later	103
Chapter Thirteen – Eggs	113
Chapter Fourteen - Caravan	123
Chapter Fifteen – Wrestling	139
Chapter Sixteen – Going Home	145
Chapter Seventeen – Jake in 1917	157
Chapter Eighteen – The Journalist	165
Chapter Nineteen – The Morning After	171
Chapter Twenty – Mushrooms	177
Chapter Twenty-One – A Few Days On	183
Chapter Twenty-Two – Nearly There	187
Chapter Twenty-Three – Her Day Arrives	201
In The Days That Followed	213
The Others Who Were There	217

Introduction

In this story as in real life, Bobcat whom you will soon know well, wandered away for two months on a long journey just a few days after he was moved with his people to a new house in a nearby town.

Bobcat, or as his people's little girl sometimes likes to call him: Bobcat-Cat the cat! He and his adopted brother Baskerville live with two adult humans called Mike and Dee, and their young daughter Annie, who as it happens had voted herself the job of being allowed to choose him from a litter of eight kittens at the beginning of his life.

Baskerville may sound to only get a walk-on part in all this, but his influence on things, and not least on Bobcat, is considerable.

Annie herself is growing up fast, but her unusual ability to feel and anticipate peoples' thoughts, and also to follow and search for things in her dreams, is growing even faster… so this book is just as much the story of a self aware and remarkable young girl… and several others who had lives lived previously in the scenery the journey inhabits and from which the echoes still reverberate.

Chapter One

Things Moving Around

It's not always easy to tell exactly what's wrong, especially if you're just a cat.

Bobcat stretches one languid long black paw across his chair as if he were reaching out to something, but there is nothing worth grabbing at and it soon falls slack across his long sphinx-like nose.

Bobcat's nose is not like most cats' noses; most cats' noses are quite short and wide with a spread of stiff white whiskers spraying out all ways; of course Bobcat has got whiskers, but they're fine and dark, and you only notice them when you get down close to him to tickle him under the chin; only as you are nuzzling him and saying 'hello little Bobbywobby' or something similarly daft, do you then realise there is something tickling your nose.

The reason why Bobcat has a long nose is because his mum is a Siamese cat and his dad a big black Manx cat, and when you put these two breeds together, their kittens always tend to have long noses.

Manx cats of course don't have a proper tail, just a little stumpy tuft that sticks up.

So why is it today that Bobcat thinks there is something wrong in his house; why does it seem to him that things are moving?

Things have gone from where they usually are; the big square pictures that usually hang on the walls have all been taken down, and are all wrapped in newspaper and packed in a large cardboard box near the top of the stairs.

The rack of kitchen plates that normally glint bright and shiny on the red wire stand by the sink are in a box now, and the red wire plate rack itself has also gone.

Lots of things began moving around a couple of days ago, and some big things even found their way down to the old glass fronted Victorian porch.

Now when Bobcat hears a door slam, or if Dee bumps her vacuum cleaner against the skirting board as she hoovers through the house there is a hollow echo in each room.

From where he is out on the landing sitting beside Annie's huge but now rather thread-bare teddy bear, still loved from when she was small, Bobcat could imagine that the bedroom Dee is cleaning has somehow grown into a big echoey church hall… well he could imagine it if he had even the slightest notion what a church hall is; he has heard the same hollow reverberation when Annie and her mates run through the courtyard outside, and the slap of their feet, and their yelps and giggles rattle off the old stable doors.

Not all of the boxes in the house have been packed with plates and stuff, there is one empty one waiting at the bottom of the stairs on which someone has written in marker pen 'Cats, (then underlined) do not kick or drop, or stack anything too heavy on top!'

If Bobcat or Baskerville could read the words written on this box it would give them a big clue about what is going on here today.

Bobcat sits with his ears twitching, and nose waffling as it looks for answers, and soon hears the ascending tump tump tump tump tump… of his adopted brother Baskerville trotting back up the stairs.

Baskerville has been down in the trees and bushy stuff beyond the garages. He likes to creep through the undergrowth and long grass, then hopefully jump on mice that venture optimistically out from under the fallen trunk of the big tree that fell down in the great storm a year or so back.

The night of the great storm had been a night when the wind howled and moaned through the tall pine trees making them bend and strain; at one side their roots pushed hard down onto and into the dry ground, on the other lifting to crumble and craze the surface. Many leant and pulled so far they wrenched free their grip on Mother Earth.

All this happened when Bobcat and Baskerville were little more than big kittens.

In that howling moaning windy night many slates were ripped from the old stables' rooftops and smashed on the cobblestones of the courtyard; and through that harried darkness serried ranks of beeches up the driveway fell across.

The wind shouted with a voice few could remember hearing before.

Baskerville and Bobcat were both outside because they were enjoying the voice of the wind that night. For the first hour it just seemed great fun, and they raced around the dark whirlwind whipped courtyard chasing the leaves and pine needles that swirled about.

The first few slates that came spinning down gave them great entertainment; Baskerville led the chase as pieces smashed and rolled, and were blown as if paper light across the courtyard.

One spinning slate came down right beside Bobcat and cut his shoulder as it smashed. He gave a sharp meow and ran in under the old car that had sat rusting for years in the door-less stable right at the end; he sat there licking his cut shoulder but in truth not really very badly hurt.

Baskerville started to worry a bit now, his fur was being blown all over the shop; he left off chasing leaves and bits and followed Bobcat into their safe corner.

Leaves continued to dance, and branches circled and swirled at a mesmerising speed; Baskerville glanced round thinking Bobcat was trying to get his attention… or that he was seeing another cat sitting between them, yet seeming to be there, and not be there at one and the same time… Bob though was utterly absorbed and watching the show, and much later we will know more about the third cat.

That was where they stayed watching the leaves and branches swirling around the yard until Dee was woken by all the wind and noise, and sent Michael out to find them and call them both in.

Long ago before there were hardly any cars in England… we mean back in the old days when fine ladies with big hats and big backsides came to visit the family in the mansion house here; after they had alighted at the grand front door round the other side their muddy and creaking coach was brought round to this courtyard to be parked in a dry shed for the night, and the horses fed and put to bed in one of the stables.

There was a young lad who worked as stable boy and handyman during the summer months of the year also as a gardener for this big old house; his name was Jake Jones and he was sixteen years old; he lived in a single attic room above the stable in the corner where the tradesmens' path goes through and round towards the kitchens and servant's quarters of the big house.

In a year's time from when we see him employed here, Jake will walk and work and scrounge his way down to Cornwall, then take up a job as handyman and gardener at a big house on the edge of the moor near Bodmin.

Three years after that, but still a long time back from this day where we all are now, Jake will join the army to fight in the 1914-18 war. He shall, I am sorry to tell you, loose his right leg to machine gun fire during a desperate and as everyone unlucky enough to be there could see, completely futile attack on a heavily armed German fortification; but that is still a few years off for him, though still more than seventy years back in the memory of the courtyard here.

He was always very happy when there were visiting horses that had pulled a carriage to the house, because they would be put straight into the straw filled stable under his floor. During the evening the heat from their big warm bodies would rise up through gaps in the floorboards to warm his loft room and the chilly roof tiles above his bed. Okay, it did sometimes make things drip with condensation rather, but at least it was not so cold.

In his room Jake had little except his bed, a small chest of drawers for the few clothes he possessed, and a heavy wooden box with a padlock where he kept his few bits and pieces, such as the stuff his granny left for him when she died two years ago.

Jake has an enamelled tin bread bin where he keeps his loaf and cheese, and sometimes a cold sausage if he can scrounge one from the kitchen girl in the main house who fancies him.

He has of course no toilet up there in the roof… well only

the same one as the horses down below. If he wants to go in the middle of the night he has to stand at the edge of the trap door and wee down into the darkness of the stable below. Sometimes a horse may whinny in complaint if he or she gets it in the ear, but mostly they sleep up the back where their food is.

Jake is half asleep when he gets up in the night so must be careful not to fall through the trap door; we know how easy it is to fall over things when you are only partly awake!

His cat Disraeli also liked it to be warm up in their room. He would lounge there beside the open hatchway where most of the heat from the horses came up.

Disraeli liked to be out hunting mice and rats too. Within a couple of hours of Jake falling asleep the cat would wake up, stretch, and reach down through the hatchway to the first step and manoeuvre backwards down the footholds cut in boarded wall of the stable.

Pausing after climbing backwards halfway down the foot holes, he will look over his shoulder at the horses, especially if they're visiting horses he doesn't know… some horses were a bit mad and would try to trample a cat if they could. Seeing none with ears held back or nostrils flared he would turn and leap to the floor and go swiftly out beneath the stable door rail.

If it was a wet night he liked to shelter under the old cart in the open stable at the end… that's right, the same open shed that Bobcat and Baskerville will take refuge in on the night of the great storm in 1987, but that's so far off in years that if any children were here now with Jake, they will be old by then; and also by then there will just be a rusty old car in the later door-less open shed.

Jake's cat peers patiently and eagerly out across the yard from his crouch beneath the old cart…

'Disraeli is a resourceful cat, and though not thin he isn't fat, but very strong,

He waits beneath that cart so patient, and his wait will not be long,

Before a small grey form with long thin tail sneaks out below a stable door rail.

And halting, this form then snuffs the air, looks up and squeaks at the moon, or was that a squeak for a lover somewhere.

Ratty thinks his path is clear and heads for a drink at the puddle where cobbles slope to a drain in the middle of the yard.

For this cunning cat it's not that hard to just pick off one stupid rat!'

'It's not that hard, to just'

But we return from those distant days far back in the memory of this courtyard; and now straight across the centre drain where that rat had his final drink trots Baskerville, and as always without a care in the world as far as you can see.

Today as Baskerville comes cantering up with his pads sounding tump tump tump to the top of the stairs, Bobcat peers inquisitively at his adopted brother to see if he knows more than he does himself about all these boxes and things; the look that returns is unconcerned, but that's just typical of Baskerville.

Everything in life is just a game to Baskerville, as long as there is food in their bowl at dinnertime… then nothing else matters.

Chapter Two

In a Box

It's fun in a box.

It's always been fun to be in a box.

Even right back when the two of them put together were still miles smaller than either one of them on its own is now, they liked being in a box.

When you're in a box you romp and fight and rip the walls, and bite your adopted brother's tail knowing he cannot bite yours because you haven't got a tail.

Then because you're still small you both fall asleep in the dingy dark. The criss-cross of light where the flaps of the box have been folded above you like the arms of two stubborn bickering women winks and blinks as your humans come and lean over and listen. Dee and Annie joke that it sounds as if the cats have eaten each other.

Last time they were in a box they were small, and now they're big.

Now being in a box tells you that it should be fun when you are first stuffed in there by your people; stuffed in there as if they are about to start some wild game with you… and you remember diving from one end to the other like some mad thing, but it seems so much smaller in a box now, and though you prepare to grab at anything that gets poked in through the various air holes, nothing happens.

Now you skulk disconsolate, of freedom lost and waiting to be let back out to light.

Crouched inside you feel heavy as someone picks the box up; after heavy you fall light, and then normal but bouncy and you lurch around as without knowing it you are carried somewhere.

Inside the box you are still crouching as you were, and your adopted brother's ears twitch as you peer inquisitively at him to see if he is making more sense of it all than you are.

So when does this wonderful game start? What have your humans got to do before they begin poking things in through the holes for you both to start grabbing at and fighting with?

Minutes on you hear and feel the bottom of the box go 'plaff' as it is put down onto… well something; what it's onto could be anything. It also sounds as if your humans have gone away from where they might otherwise have begun playing and poking bits in through the air holes.

All you can do now is wait until… well, who can say when or what for; you wait for quite some time there in the dark, and looking into each other's luminous green eyes for clues… like can the other perhaps see why we are in a box but not as yet being played with?

Other changes occur, as with a clanging rattle and the sound which you have never heard like grumbling school buses when all the kids have just got into their seats shakes the box, and it continues to shake a bit because this rumble keeps going.

Then their box moves again, has it been picked up so their humans can take them where they can play with them? The shaking is joined by lurch and movement, and the rumble and crunch of wheels or something; must be some sort of new game they have not played before.

Dee and Annie have driven off in the little car borrowed from Granny, and gone on ahead to unlock the new house. Yes that's what the boys in the box don't realise, the family is moving house today.

Granny said the box of cats must travel in the van because she didn't want her seats spoiled if they wetted through the bottom of their box!

The women went on a little while ago so they could first go round to the front of this big house and hand the old key back in to the landlord.

I wonder what our two furry boys in this box think is going on; probably that it's just some kind of game and so they're still just waiting for it to start to be fun.

It's time to get going; the sooner they get over to the new house the sooner they can be out the box and exploring their new world.

The jolting and lurching has gone on for quite a while.

The cats in the box are thinking (or what passes for thought in a cat's head) that if this bumping and shaking is all the game is going to involve, it will not be as much fun as some of the others they have played with their humans.

Just now and then one or other of them will turn and look up at a hole in the box to see if something is about to be poked in.

Like some cancelled football-match, or even just one with a delayed 'kick-off' their box rattles and jolts along while inside they wait for the whistle to start things off; this motion feels like the preparation for a sudden arrival of fun and games and wild scrabbling with paws and claws… that does not come.

Sometimes all falls still, and the rattling falls silent, but it's only because they have stopped at traffic lights, but the boys are sure it is because someone is just about to start shoving things to fight with in through a hole in their box… that does not happen either.

After quite a while of grinding and lurching they feel the box tilt while the moaning noise stays quite high but all stops quickly with a lurch and falls silent.

Their box remains still; outside their box there is bumping and rocking and voices of their humans laughing and telling each other to get on with things, 'you come and lift it from this end Dee', and 'no… we'll never get through like that' and then, 'mind your knuckles as we go in through the gate'.

At one point the cats go heavy for a few moments and the light through the holes goes funny and flickers a bit; then feeling drowsy and a little fed up they both doze off for a while in the warm dark air of the box.

It is with some surprise and questioning glances when they are roused to a settled homely tone of music, a CD perhaps… no, it's a television.

Well that all seemed a bit daft; as far as they can tell they've just been put in a box, and the box has been put in something that makes a rumbling sound and shakes around a lot, then after a lot of nothing very much they've been carried back into their house again.

What was the point of shutting them into a box and then not playing games with them; then when the humans want to watch their TV they bring them back into the house as if nothing had happened… they hear flap and flip, and shards of daylight cut across their drowsy heads as spread the flaps of box are pulled apart… the world reopens.

You are out of the box at last, and being two cats who are both eager to get on with having some fun you leap straight into action. In front of you is your big familiar yellow sofa which you bound towards then swerve sharp left and start to race each other but with your claws trying to get a grip on the suddenly different feeling floor.

The cats always compete to be the first up onto their favourite table. As you gather feet to make your jump you see that for some reason it is just the television in front of you and if you jump you are going to shoot straight over the back and into the wall.

You skid to a halt in front of the television and young Annie squeals at you in her high little 'would-be pop-star' singing voice, while her eyes shine like happy stars… she can see what you were both thinking you were about to jump up onto.

Since you were big enough to do it she has loved watching you bounce across the floor and then fly up onto the table down the end of the sitting room. She loves the way you skid across the shiny polished top and only just stop as you get to the other end.

But here in this new house, and with both cats thinking their box was just carried back into the normal house, they think that same table has now been put at the other end of the sitting room by the window, but as the cats spin round and try and make sense of things they can see that the window that has always been halfway along the long side of the room is now at one narrow end; nor is it matched with the position of the door and the sofa.

This is going to take some working out; so the boys sit down and curl their tails round over their front paws to think… no that's not true is it, only Baskerville can do that, Bobcat just has to sit on his little stumpy tail.

But they can both do the next thing that cats like to do when they feel a bit unsure of things; they both start washing one paw… when that paw is nice and wet they use it to rub over the back of their silky ear and over the side of their face. They re-lick the paw all the time they are doing it so they can taste when there is no more dust or old food to wash off. With the first side finished of course they just start again on the other side.

By the time they have washed their whole face they feel calm and collected, and ready to begin trying to make some sense of their altered surroundings.

You're just a cat, so you never do make sense of your altered surroundings, nor even try; as the minutes tick by you just start looking for stuff to do, things to get up to; how the room is now just gets included in what you do as you start doing it.

You do need to go round doing a lot of sniffing, there are so many new smells to be sniffed at.

As a cat you have no idea why the house is now so changed, or why the smells are all so different. Being in a new place is not a concept that your mother bothered to teach you… nor knew herself the chances are.

In not very long you have found where the stairs have been moved to and you go running up to find the beds; when you find the bath has been moved into one of your bedrooms you are surprised, but it has the sort of smell you expect to smell, except seems to have changed in some way that your sort of memory does not record; could it be that the bath has changed colour as well?

Baskerville has sloped off, and is quickly at home in this altered house; he is now dozing off on one of the beds and purring quietly like he has slept in this room all his life. He has slept on this bed many times before, but in a room with just one window, and with a low ceiling that slopes from just above the bed.

Baskerville wouldn't notice all of that; he is a cat that worries about… well about nothing really, he just gets on with it wherever he finds he is. Of course for a cat, getting on with it can mean just falling asleep on a bed.

Bobcat on the other hand sneaks quietly up the stairs looking sideways and suspiciously through the landing rails as he tip-toe's onto the top stair. All seems quiet, and the coast seems clear so he sneaks into the first bedroom and the bed seems familiar so that's a good start; maybe he is in the right place after all.

He puts his paws up on the edge of the bed to investigate and gets the shock of his life! There is another cat asleep on the bed. Now this is terrible, and where is his adopted brother to help him at a time like this. Then the drowsing cat lifts his head and Bobcat jumps back thinking he is under attack… and sees it is just Baskerville.

Bobcat feels like a bit of a dumpling for not realising who it really was, but Baskerville just puts his chin down and dozes off again.

'Well' he sort of thinks, 'if he can just go to sleep on a bed then I can too.' Bobcat is up and curling himself into a ball near the other cat; and if he had one his tail would be curled round over his nose.

Chapter Three

Jake Jones

For two or three muggy scented nights the cats have been kept in; well there has been no cat-flap for them to slip out through to explore the dark, and each fizzing squeak of zoomed bat or gourmet snuffle of worming hedgehog outside brought them alert and expectant to the kitchen garden door.

During the day Dee has let them come outside with her a few times just onto the lawn while she gets some washing in or hangs some more out.

To the cats the garden seems to have changed as much as does this house. Perhaps when they eventually get to go out in the night it will seem back to its old self again.

So that they can go to the toilet in the night Dee has put a big green litter tray full of chalky granules near the door that would lead out into the garden. The cats don't really mind using it, but it would be far more fun if they could to be going out into the dark for relief and a sniff around; sometimes while they sniff around they will meet a hedgehog as he or she comes snuffling across the lawn hunting juicy worms. The fun relationship you can have with a hedgehog is really rather limited it must be said, but all the same you find no objection to hedgehogs because at least they don't bark at you or chase you out of what they think is 'their garden'.

Gardens at night are also nice because sometimes there is a bold little mouse or vole or shrew sizzling and squeaking and begging to be jumped on along the stony bank where you have stopped to sniff the drooping scented head of a half closed pansy before you pee on it.

Gardens at night have various high bits that you leap up onto. You jump like a furry jack-in-the-box onto one of your favourite big corner fence posts perhaps; from up there you look across into the dark but glowing flowerbeds of the next garden. The lupins glimmer luminous and yellowy green like organic mobile phones on stems.

As the hooting great white floppy feathered barn owl flaps through trees, and cuts across the end of your garden, you are not afraid when his big eyes fix on you, but you still lower your head a little just in case he comes too close for comfort.

You want to be out in the garden at night again so you can get back to things that all your life you loved to sniff or pad, or pounce or grab… to the places where your happiness has been.

It would perhaps have been just such a night as this one, except years and years earlier, and while the sun is not yet set; on this night so far behind us, Jake Jones does not need to be early to bed because he does not have to get up to work tomorrow.

He is lounging on an old kitchen chair that was discarded by the butler in the main house; one that has been repaired with string so many times that it would better be chucked on the fire. He tilts nonchalantly back in the corner of the courtyard as he swigs his lovely mug of tea, his week's work done. He is probably hoping that a couple of the kitchen girls may wander through this way on the evening garden stroll that they often take at the weekend.

It is always a late stroll that they take because they must be sure that all the ladies and gentlemen have gone inside for the evening; the lord and master of the house does not like to see staff wandering about the grounds until the gentry have all gone inside for the evening. Often they are sent indoors by fear of catching a chill as the dew forms freshly distilled on the grass.

But Jake has made himself a cup of tea on the coal burning stove in the mower shed in the corner of the courtyard. Up in his stable attic he is not allowed to have a stove because of the fire risk; his employers do not really like him having even a candle to undress by when he goes to bed. The only hot food and drinks that Jake gets are what he knocks together in the mower shed, or what he manages to scrounge from the girls in the kitchens.

The lawn mower shed of course has a little chimney on the top, and as there were no mowers driven by petrol back in the early nineteen hundreds it's pretty safe.

The machines that the gardeners use are heavy green metal ones, and they need one big man to push and steer, and two strong young boys pulling with their shoulders through a leather harness like horses pulling a cart.

Reclining outside on his tilting chair, that looks like if he isn't careful not to twist around could let him down badly; but tilting there with his mug of tea he hears a sound he loves, and it's the sound of young female feet tapping on the flagstones as they get near, and the friendly trilling of raised voices like bird song calling out to attract a mate.

Though he's fairly sure he knows the bodies that are likely to be joined to the tapping feet, Jake leans a little forward to see for sure that one of them is definitely going to be the one he fancies.

As he tilts, and they come through, the legs explode! (not hers or hers or his of course!) with showers of splintered matchwood, and both girls stop and stand framed with mouths aghast in the courtyard's stone archway.

27

You hear a millisecond later the sound of Jake's china mug smashing into a thousand jigsaw pieces on the stones of the courtyard, and he shouts out what sounds something like being about 'ducks' and a 'bell' as his legs fly in the air.

The girls dissolve in laughter, but then gasp and run quickly and a tadge eagerly over to where he lies groaning and deliberately trying to look injured to disguise his embarrassment. The pretty faced chubby one is quick to get down to him:

"Oh Jake you poor thing, are you alright?"

"I'm not quite sure"

He hisses breathily, dragging a look of pain and toughness across his face; the slim one clearly wants to do her bit as a caring nurse as well, and pulls at the shoulder of her chubby friend with an eager,

"I was the first aid captain in our church youth group so I know the proper way to check for injuries Alice, let me see a minute."

"This is more like it"

Jake thinks to himself (This is the one he was sitting there hoping to see come past). What a stroke of luck his chair decided to collapse just when it did; just imagine if it had held together till they had gone through, it would all have been wasted; he would have lost his china mug and all its tea, his rickety old chair, his pride... but most of all, the chance to be fussed over by Mary!

"Okay Jake I'm just going to take your pulse…"

"Well what's the flipping point of that Mary, he's just fallen off his chair not passed out or anything!"

"No but you still check it Alice so that it can be crossed off the list then you know where you are starting from."

"Okay then, just get on with it."

You can tell there is some rivalry between these two. Jake is a good looking lad, and word among all the kitchen staff and maids in the big house is that he would be a good catch for some lucky girl. As soon as that sort of word gets put about girls will compete to prove that they could have him if they wanted; even the ones who live up in the village where they have the pick of lots of boys find they are making sparkly eyes at Jake.

Mary continues:

"Yes it's okay Jake, you have got a pulse…"

"Well of course he has you silly moo, or he would be dead by now with all your farting about!"

"I didn't finish, I was going to add that his pulse seems pretty strong and regular."

Mary is still holding the hand that she had taken his pulse

from, and notices that if anything the pulse has quickened quite a lot and become stronger… and in his eyes, a deep dilation settles.

Alice feeling a bit out of the action has nipped round the other side to soothe his brow which still holds that furrowed look of grim determination not to be beaten by the pain of his apparent injuries.

Jake realises it is down to him to pull some new idea into the scene if he wants to keep them fussing over him.

He begins to raise himself then suddenly winces and gasps and falls back again.

"Ah you poor thing be careful, don't start trying to move too soon."

"Yeah thanks Mary… yes and er Alice too; but my back is hurting and I feel hot and a little breathless… I wonder what I've done?"

"If you're hot and breathless I must undo your shirt Jake, hang on…"

"no it's okay Mary, I can do it more easily from over here."

"Well alright then Alice but mind you don't jerk him about, I still can't be sure he hasn't broken his back!"

"Don't panic, I'm only undoing his naffing buttons!"

"Right Jake, we need to be certain that you haven't broken your back… (and she still has hold of his hand) Alice will go down to your feet to see if they move at all when I give the word for you to try."

"So why can't you go down to watch his flipping feet Mary, I've got to mop his brow for him."

"No Alice, I em… I must check to feel if there is a change in his pulse when he tries to move his feet."

Alice would rather stick with mopping his fevered brow, but rises reluctantly and takes up an unenthused position at his feet.

She thinks to herself that you can't use much passion watching a pair of blasted feet; nor can you imagine yourself as Florence Nightingale worshipped by the injured soldiers as you go up and down the darkened wards with your lamp at night.

She crouches by the large rough booted feet and wonders whether she should be trying to soothe them or something. How with great thick leather hob-nailed boots can she stroke or soothe them or stand any chance to stake her equal claim on attention with Jake… Alice has a sudden brain wave…

"Hey I've just thought Mary… if it's only his toes that twitch, I will not see them, shall I take one of his boots off?"

"Well yes, I suppose if you are careful not to pull at his leg Alice."

Her eager fingers twiddle excitedly at his laces and she whips his boot off as if she has been undressing men all her life. The smell of his foot hits her in a hurricane of rotten cheese, and about half her young womanly passion retreats back into her hitherto eager heated body.

"Holy mother Mary Jake, how long have you had these socks on for?"

"They're new Alice, those were a Christmas present from the butler's wife."

"But we're in the end of May now Jake!"

"Yes I know the sock is a bit stiff and scratchy with cheese but my foot inside is okay, I went into the bathhouse as I finished work this afternoon."

"Then I think I'll just pull your sock off Jake."

Now this starts to feel more like she is emulating her heroine nurse because she's got a proper bit of body to do something with.

Alice is about to ask if she should do anything with Jake's foot when she realises the answer is bound to be no from Mary, so she keeps quiet and starts by just holding it. If Mary says it doesn't need to be held she will say she is getting ready to feel for muscle flutter in case he can't quite actually move it.

Alice can hear Mary saying something to Jake in a deliberately soothing voice about 'it's okay now' and then 'but not too quickly Jake' and 'don't try too hard now'.

Mary turns to Alice down at the feet end saying,

"Is there any movement yet Alice?"

"It's a bit hard to say because my head is still spinning from smelling his revolting cheesy socks! But not really at the movement, except perhaps I think I felt a twinge once or twice."

She adds to ensure she doesn't talk herself out of the job.

Rather than wait for her friend to throw a new command down to her Alice has a thought and,

"They may need some gentle help… I shall massage them very gently to bring them back to life."

She takes a gamble as she throws in 'I shall' instead of 'shall I?'

"Hmm… alright then Alice, as long as you are gentle now!"

Finally Alice has snatched the initiative away from her first aid expert friend, and she begins to rub and stroke the sole and top of Jake's foot.

He lies there and continues looking grim and pained as long as he can, and wanting to carry on the idea of maybe having sustained paralysis and loss of feeling from the waist down. Gradually the corners of his mouth start to twitch and lift and his chin starts to quiver; his tummy twitches and bounces up and down a little till he has to give in to the tickling of his foot and he hoots and cackles like a turkey.

The spell has been broken and they all know the act must now be relinquished.

After the two girls have waited while he puts his sock and boot back on, and even both helped to pull him to his feet from amongst the wood of the smashed chair, they say goodbye and wander off.

As they amble on round the garden Mary thinks to herself:

"I'm sure Jake stayed on the ground because he liked having me looking after him; it's a shame I hadn't been out on my own tonight."

Alice's thoughts are much the same.

"I could feel how he liked having his brow soothed. I hope it didn't annoy him too much when Mary was trying to fiddle with his pulse and stuff."

So we leave these girls to wander off through their employer's fine big garden all those years ago, and we come flying back to the present where the cats are waiting to be allowed to go out into their new garden at night… while we are all in bed *(though they will probably expect to find it's somehow still the old garden)*.

Chapter Four

Her Dream

Leaving Jake and his girls to get on with things back at the start of the 'nineteen hundreds', we have come back to today... and today as you slept on beds, or wandered around to check for other stuff to do... or to eat, there has been the grinding and drilling and swearing sound of your dad-person working away at the back door; then sawing and taking some of it out in a square shape.

It doesn't really tell you what he's doing because you're just a cat.

You have no way of knowing that it isn't just going to go back to how it was when he stops doing it. You have of course been enjoying the smells of the garden though it; they come wafting and tantalising past his hunched and grumbling form.

It makes both of you jump back a bit as his screwdriver slips off the screw head and stabs into his thumb and he yells "oh shoogaluubadooba!" He pretends to cry, and Dee has to come and cuddle his face against her warm soft snugly front, which always helps to shut him up.

As evening spreads across the sky, and birds to east and west fly high beneath the golden glow of their enormous ceiling; the cats are still up on the beds with their tummies rising up and down like half deflated bouncy castles where the kids all jump together in slow motion.

The cats dream perhaps of jumping on a mouse as it runs from under a flowerpot, and their whiskers twitch as if in their minds they were about to do something really exciting… but their tummies just go dreamily up and down with every breath.

What they hear next might just be part of a dream yet doesn't fit with what either of them is dreaming about. It comes again… first their ears point and twist, then both lift their head with big round staring eyes:

"Come on you boys, come for a play in the garden."

It's Dee's voice floating up from below.

Even though they don't know the actual words they know the tone means there is some sort of fun going on somewhere and they are invited to join in.

Bobcat and Baskerville sit up on the bed and at the same time see where the voice has come from in the garden, for there as they look out the bedroom window are Dee and her moderately *(he would say very!)* handsome husband Michael right down the lawn and heading for the little summerhouse at the end of the garden.

Like two coiled springs they shoot off the bed and down the stairs. They somehow know this means they have their freedom at last. Then it's a gallop down the hall and into the kitchen to shoot out the back door: which is shut.

The boys skid to a halt; what a swiz to be called down to play and then only to find their way is barred, but at least there's now a window in the door now so they can look out and see if mum is coming back to let them out.

Dee looks up the garden from down the end; she can see

two little staring faces with four big pleading eyes that want to be outside having fun in the evening light. She smiles at the sight of their desperate little faces and waves to them calling,

"Bobbykins, Baskin, why don't you both come out here to have a game on the lawn?"

They know she is calling them out by the tone of her words and the way she swings her arm as she looks up the garden at them; both lift their heads in expectation like otters.

Baskerville is always the fastest to get to the root of any problem and he leaves their little window in the door and has a quick shifty round the kitchen to check they haven't missed some vital clue to all this that can win them their freedom.

There are no windows open above and no new door that he has previously overlooked, so he returns quickly to their little door window and stands up on his hind legs to put his paws up and his nose against it to shout out to his mum person.

It is with some surprise that he finds the little plastic window has pushed away from him though not right open; it is still sitting on his paws but now his pads can feel the cool of the evening air outside, and to his ears the high-borne windy song of swifts and martins from through the small gap.

Baskerville sniffs at this gap and smells cut grass and honeysuckle carried on a lingering waft of evening breeze; so he leans more forward to get a better snuff at the world he so loves and would like to be outside in... the plastic window moves even further away.

Bobcat sits back and watches the every move his adopted brother makes; he knows that if anyone can gain them their freedom it will be Baskerville, he always was the cat to make things happen.

Dee clicks her fingers and calling up to the house,

"You're almost out now Baskin."

Hearing his name he looks up again, and as his nose feels a bump the plastic window swings out and away and thinking it's his only chance he's through and away across the lawn.

One out and one still to go; Bobcat pads his four feet keenly forward as the swinging door flicks past the magnet slowing down; he puts his paws up on the edge and the door swings down and bounces on them as if it doesn't really have to shut, so he thrusts his nose against it and remarkably it moves away from him.

A cat can learn how to do something from watching another cat, but not quite in the same way that a teacher might show you how to do things; with a cat it is much more that they see something is possible, and fiddle with it or push against it until they find it has worked for them too.

Bobcat fiddles and nuzzles the plastic window and it seems to be opening itself. The garden opens in front of him and he's through and lolloping like a mad March hare down the green lawn to get to his mum and dad.

Just before he gets down there, and as he is passing the first bushes of the little shrubbery Baskerville leaps from behind a bush and pounces on him, so they roll and tumble through the flowerbed with their mum person yelling,

"Hey you two, you mind those daffodils, we've only just moved into this nice new garden, and I don't want to see you cats wrecking it for us!"

But the boys just ignore her and carry on whacking at each other until they have fallen back out of the daffodils and onto the path. Bobcat chases Baskerville back up the lawn and trying to grab his tail as they swerve to left and right and leap up into and back out of the wheelbarrow.

They are both so happy.

They are both so happy to see their world grow back from just being a house, into being a garden as well again.

A chipping chiding blackbird goes ping ping ping as it eyes them from the metal hip-tile stay on next-door's roof. The last people here had a little Jack Russell terrier who yapped and snapped at anyone or anything he could, but never came close to catching a bird. Mind you, the reason the local birds had for not liking him was that when he was let out for his morning widdle he went straight to scoff anything that had just been put out for all the garden birds' breakfasts.

So ping ping ping, ping ping ping, and a last ping, the blackbird having carried on then stops on that single angry shout. He thinks perhaps these cats are passing through the garden on their way somewhere, and so if he keeps his scolding going and ruins the peace of their evening they will soon get the message that they are not wanted round here… at least, not by any of the birds that the blackbird might be squawking for.

But seeing these cats still playing in the garden as the darkening sky softens toward mauve, and the first damp breath of moist night air lingers around the leaves of the hedge; seeing this the scolding bird though hardly bright can sense that they will be here for a while so swoops with whirr of wing across the garden walls and dew hung washing lines. If he goes where he can't see them he won't feel that he has to keep shouting at them.

Soon all folk go inside.

As evening stars come winking bright, and twilight softens toward night,

And Dee has long since gone to watch her telly, and Michael snores in chair with heaving belly.

She stirs from chair to call the cats, 'hey boys, you want some food?' and through their flap they clatter in.

It seems they've twigged that they are free to come and go at will, and being at will, will go back out when they have scoffed their fill.'

Dee pops the ring pull and peels the lid then forks the tin of meat into their bowl. Two eager hungry heads plunge in and scoff like wolves; she smiles and goes back through to her new sitting room wondering if Annie is sleeping peacefully in her freshly painted room; later in the night will she will wake to go to the toilet and find that her wall is now on this side of the bed not that side as it was before when she woke in the night.

Annie sleeps with a very old Buzz Lightyear sat resolute and staring confidently from the left side of her pillow, while Woody gapes wide-eyed in the darkness on the right.

In her young dreams she can see Bobcat far away, not safe by fire with Mum and Dad, here he is not playing with Baskerville and running round in circles in his garden; he has gone over the fence and set off in a straight line to the next distant hedge… Annie dreams she is calling him to come back but he cannot hear her call, or just does not turn his head to see it's her, but pads away until he's out of sight.

Annie scared that she will lose him calls for mum to help but her voice won't come out and she is crying and waving at the distant bushes where he went.

But Dee hears a cry from downstairs and goes quickly up…

"hey Babes, what's up lovey… what's upset you; were you scared at being in the dark in a new room on your own sweetie?"

"No Mum it's Bobcat… he's gone through the hedge and how ever much I called him he took no notice of me and carried on, so quickly Mum, can you call him back for me?"

"It's okay Annie he's with me downstairs… and Basky too, they've both just had their dinner and settled down in front of the fire by my feet… do you want to come back down for a little while Annie?"

"It's okay Mum, if it was just a dream it doesn't matter then, and anyway, Bobby looked like he knew where he was going; he wasn't scared or anything Mum."

Dee settles her down again with some more words exchanged about Bobcat, and gives her a kiss before going quietly down the stairs to the sitting room.

"What was up love… did Annie think she was in the wrong house maybe, or was it the dark or something?"

"No certainly not the dark, you know our Annie, she's not afraid of anything; hey can you remember even that time last year when we went wandering through that forest in Scotland in the middle of the night she wanted to wander off on her own didn't she?"

"Yeah you're right, with all the wind moaning in those big black pine trees it was really scary, and you and me were practically pooing ourselves weren't we, but trying to look brave, while she was running off through the forest like some little fairy… or goblin more like!"

"Absolutely… but no, here what it was is that in her dream Bobcat set off across the next garden I think… she was calling him back over the garden fence but he carried on away from her, she said that he seemed to know where he was going and wouldn't respond to her voice.

"As far as I could tell she was scared by the way he went, and as he was going just seemed to stop knowing her voice… I don't know Mike, but it sounded something like that is what was happening in her dream… she could see him, but he had stopped wanting to know her and just carried on away from her."

"I don't know much about all this sort of thing Dee. Can it mean she is frightened of something else that this all represents?"

"So like what?"

"Don't ask me; I suppose some weird subconscious insecurity… you know, like people all seem to have in America."

"Hmm, well I suppose it could be. Do you know what I think it was love?"

"No I don't think I really want to hear… you're going to say that I've been hurting her or bullying her aren't you?"

"Well perhaps you have, but I reckon she was just having a dream…"

"well yeah I suppose…"

'Wind tossed and moon bright…'

'And calling blackly in that wind there was a voice that said,

Beware all cats or children who are not in bed,

Watch out all owls who try to fly through trees wind tossed and moon bright,

If you fly into one beak first the grateful mice will laugh their heads off... so stay in bed tonight.'

Chapter Five

First Night Under the Stars

The telly's off:

Even the little white dot that can sometimes stay like a tiny distant risen evening star in the middle of the screen, has gone to bed.

Michael and Dee can still be heard upstairs going from room to room as they use the bathroom and check Annie has her snug duvet up over her shoulders.

Dee is first into bed. You hear the gruff tones we cannot quite make out of Mike asking her if she wants something (that means he was coming back down anyway)... then he comes creaking back down the stairs and through the quiet sitting room to the kitchen.

Both boys look up big eyed as he walks through, and he speaks a few words down to them so they crease their faces up and smile at the sound of his voice.

He goes on into the kitchen.

A cupboard opens with clink of glass; the boys know there will be no pop or rip from ring-pull can of cat-food for them; this is a human mission he is on.

They watch his naked form go back out beaker in hand and tackle a-jiggle through their room, and closing the door behind him into the hallway. Then domp domp domp his feet ascend the stairs again. Their eyes and ears trace his step as he pads across the ceiling over-head.

There is twang of spring and creak as the bed braces itself and grunts objection beneath the extra weight.

The hardly needed fire just a glimmer in the still warm hearth… above a sudden titter and a squeal as if someone is being tickled or getting cold hands put on them, then 'hmm mm mm' in deeper tone to closing movement and a warm sigh.

'The house is quiet.

Darkness clothes the silence as a glove.

The walls stand glazed in the final gloaming blush from dying coals.

Annie dreams of forests and a search that she is making,

Sends her endless restless thought on a journey she is taking.'

In her dream now at last she has caught up with Bobcat who had gone far ahead of her; now she is travelling with him through strange lands. Annie feels he has a mental sight of where he seeks; something ahead of him that must be found, but where it is, is not clear.

Downstairs in front of the fire, Bobcat lifts his head as if spoken to, or like he is tuning in to someone's thought; in his own mind he sees another place that he so loved to be at night; in his little heart he longs to be there now; it must be out there somewhere like it always was.

He looks across at Baskin as if an answer may lie with him; Baskerville lies stretched out with his head almost face up so that his ears look like a couple of black and white coal scuttles in the final gloaming of the fire.

He stands up… Bobcat that is; Bobcat stands up with the remembered scent of the world outside lifting his nose towards the door, and the need to wee now tickles him between the legs.

He speaks to his adopted brother with a little wheezy 'purrp' and leans forward to sniff his face; in answer Baskin puts one paw up to the side of Bobcat's face and licks his nose.

He stops mid lick and is asleep again.

Bobcat pads toward the door to the back garden; going through the kitchen he stops by their food bowl and finds there are still the remnants of their tea to be finished off so he sets about it; he laps some water to clear his throat and clean his chops.

Baskerville hears the cat-flap swing and rouses from his snooze to see if anyone is coming in… silence reigns in the kitchen and the house, so he nods off.

The inverted cavernous bowl of the inky sky is stabbed with a million points of flickered light, as one lonely shooting star streaks past his sight and his eyes dart up and across to trace its path.

He knows that here was where he played and tussled with his adopted brother as mum and dad laughed at their antics and scolded them for squashing daffodils; so where is that place outside the home that he has always known that he really loves and often goes? If not in here it must be just beyond that fence… or through that hedge.

His preference is to go and peer through the hedge that meanders down the side of the garden, though Jumping up on the fence down the end is rather public and shows the world he's up to something, so yes, he heads across the lawn towards the side hedge.

He walks like a cat who is increasingly sure what he is after… though not yet sure where exactly to look for it.

For a cat it is easy to slide through where the roots craze and lift the crumbly dry earth below the lowest twigs and leaves of the hedge. At the other side Bobcat peeps out and sees just another expanse of lawn… except there down the end; yes that row of small trees has a familiar outline, somewhere beyond there must be the place he always loved so much.

On arrival down the end he sniffs the trunk of the nearest small tree where he likes to rub his chin on the rough bark. He can always smell his own scent again the following night, with usually that of a slinky tortoise-shell female who comes up across the gardens from the farm out on the lane, so he is looking for the freshness of her scent today.

To his surprise it is not there at all; even if she has not been for a couple of days you can still taste it faintly… why not tonight? Through the fence across a grassy rise are the distant outlines of more trees, it could be these instead.

This grassy rise is not a lawn but deep grass like a field of hay, and wet with dew and littered here and there with discarded drink cans, and he meanders through this damp wasteland to the nearest tree to rub and sniff, but recoils at the acrid breath of dogs piss, so carries on past.

The grassy rise is now descent, and benches stand a cinder path along. The slope and the path help Bob achieve an anxious trot, then there below the third bench down is a red and white box with a most appetising smell wafting across from it.

One eager nose shoved in finds plenty of chips that he is not hungry enough to bother with, plus a lot of bones, but a fair few scraps of tasty chicken too.

For one moment Bob thinks he's at home with his nose in his bowl of food, but there would also be his brother's nose thrust in beside.

He pulls back from the box and looks round… where is his brother now? Yes he's at their home… and with their mum and dad people, and their little girl person; it's round here somewhere isn't it, he has just come from there… but the 'there' he came from was a bit strange anyway; there were plenty of the same things that his home always had, but not all where you are used to them being.

Feeling a little nervous and exposed he thinks it's time to go back inside and check on his adopted brother, maybe Baskin will come back out to show him where he's going wrong; Baskerville always sorts things out for him and shows the way.

All above and around the stars wink down.

It is as if you are inside an enormous dark balloon and someone has thrown a handful of glitter up to adhere through static electricity all around inside high above your head.

Sloping away from him is a glimmering fall of dewy grass, and the cinder path disappears off between dark scratchy walls of tangled hawthorn on the side of a shallow valley.

Looking the other way there are houses and gardens. Bobcat scans these roofs and lights and gardens to fix his sights on the right combination of shapes that will be his home or at least the way home.

He can see nothing.

Not nothing as in an absence of anything there.

He looks out from his little grassy hill at all the house shapes… and none of them is his. None has any shape or shade or detail that he knows. He has never needed to or in passing learned to trace his route to get home again and has not tonight made any mental note of where he's been.

When he goes out from his home at night just everywhere he is he knows; it's never been anything like this, with all this, 'things around you that you've never seen before' sort of stuff.

He doesn't know the idea or possibility of not finding things. When you know in your head what you are looking for it must be there somewhere so you keep looking and it must appear sooner or later.

A cat cannot reason that out of the four opposite directions you might go searching, three of them are definitely wrong; and that you need a very good reason to head off along whichever one you choose. It is as if he thinks that whichever direction he chooses, if you search hard enough you are bound to find what you are after.

Bobcat doesn't like the idea of all those roads of houses. The starlit grassy hillside with the cinder path going into the quiet darkness of the valley looks much more his sort of place, and the sort of place where he wants his people to live.

A long anxious Siamese nose with its dark whiskers twitching nervously points along the path, then with a worried meow he pads away into the dark.

Chapter Six

Biff

"Wakey wakey Annie".

The sky outside is clear and blue, though a horizon away big puffy whites are building on the shimmered sea.

"Did you sleep well lovey, after your little dream about Bobcat?"

From their roof that blackbird sings out again, like a choir of adolescent boys, and sees no cats that he must scold today.

"Yes Mum, but I went a long way with Bobcat when I found him last night."

"What do you… yes I see now love, you had a dream that you went to look after Bobby did you?"

"He's looking for somewhere Mum so I went a long way with him so that if need be I could help him to cross roads and things."

"Well that was very kind of you Annie, I expect he'll say thank you when you see him down stairs love."

"But he can't be down there, he's miles away!"

"Well Baskerville was eating breakfast as I came to wake you up Annie, I think Bobcat must be in the garden round the back."

"No he's not Mum."

"Well if he doesn't appear we'll go and call him in when you're dressed."

Dee is slightly unsettled by the informed tone and the way her daughter told her that Bobcat has gone.

As she is getting Annie's school clothes from her cupboards she steals a glance out of the bedroom window, keenly hoping to see Bobcat sleeping in the wheelbarrow or up on the flat shed roof so she can point him out to Annie.

The garden is devoid of cats.

Even when she hears the swinging cat-flap signalling that Baskerville has had his food, and sees him padding out into the sun no deadly ambush gets him from behind the shrubs.

Dee sees him staring up and down and sniffing the wind like a cat who has lost something, though if not quite that, then a cat who feels some absence from his life.

Yes strange she thinks to hear her girl say all she has and Bobcat not be out there in the sun; or skulking there beneath the hedge to pounce on bird. Perhaps that swinging cat-flap was one out and one in, and he's down there scoffing his food right now.

"What do you fancy for socks today love… one black and one white or both the same!"

"Oh don't be silly, we've got a visit to an old people's home today, they will laugh if I have one of each… will they all be as old as you Mum?"

"Oy you watch it young lady, you know I'm only thirty two!"

"But is there anywhere between being that and being a granny?"

"Right let's get you dressed shall we?"

Dee tugs the clothes around in mock annoyance at her daughter's cheeky quip and gives her a dig in the ribs as she helps her on with her vest.
Annie is quite old enough to get herself up and dress herself. Dee likes to do it with her because Annie as her only child, is also still her baby too.
As a shirt follows the vest a promise is made to have a quick look round for the cat before they head off to the school.
Annie smiles at her mum and says okay, but in a way says it as if she is saying it just to humour Dee.

They are nearly ready to go and have some breakfast now. Dee is putting stuff back into a draw and she asks Annie where her school shoes are, and learns that Dad left them downstairs after he polished them last night; they both go down.

This day is dry and bright as Bobcat wakes.

Back in the night he had stopped at an old fallen tree and dozed for a while where its upturned roots made a little dry chalky ledge with a roof of lifted turf; then moving on before the sun climbed cold and milky behind him Bob came to a little river; he drank plenty before following its ambling path up the valley.

So now he is waking for a second time in his first night, but this time what he found just looked like a garden shed though there was no house right nearby. There was a big house standing among tall Scots Pines some way off up a grassy slope, but he had come in from the woodland footpath past the end of their big garden and was hardly aware of there being a house there at all.

His interest had been in the little shed that he discovered had a cut away corner to its door, so through he crept. Inside the smell was dusty and damp, but close and friendly with the warm woody oil of garden chairs, and damp earthy tang of gardening gloves, and musty old coats… best of all there was an old fruit box half full of rags.

Bob had made his nest in all the rags and passed a peaceful second half to his night's sleep… or third sleep if you count when he was dozing in front of the fire at home with Baskerville.

So it is about the same time that Dee and Annie are setting off to school that Bobcat who may well have carried on dreaming and dozed a while longer, is suddenly assaulted by an ear splitting howling not more than a metre from his box.

He spins over onto his front like a cat who has fallen off a table and his claws are out ready to either leap or fight. He crouches in the box and peers with desperate eyes through the gap between its strips of wood as the howling howls louder and higher, but still not nearer.

Now he can see through to the cut out corner of the shed door where the enormous nose of a monstrous dog has been thrust in. It howls and sniffs, then howls again and sniffs some more which causes it to howl even louder.

It is just as well there is a padlock on the door, he would have forced it open by now if there were just the little lifty catch bit.

The sort of brain that a cat has tells it to stand its ground, while at the same time it looks quickly about for an escape route. He scans quickly up the back wall then down to both corners. There is nothing like the hole he came in through… except 'the hole he came in through', but that's got some horrible baying bloodhound stuffing his great ugly nose through it.

As fast as it arrived the dog has suddenly gone quiet… or even gone. The absence of hoots and howls is almost worse than… hoots and howls, so where has the cursed thing gone? Is it sneaking round the back to make a rear guard lunge, or cunning flanker from the side, where will those howls assault from next…

… But why would a huge great killer hound suddenly go quiet?

They never just get bored with things because like a cat they just haven't got enough brain to get bored that easily. There is also now another warbling sound that's coming down the grassy slope towards the shed.

It's a woman's voice.

Here calling a word that means nothing to Bobcat, but there is undoubtedly a connection with the dog's disappearance.

Bob just remains rooted to the spot. His desperate claws have sown themselves like needles into the top layer of rags, and if he had made a run for it he would have looked as if he was dragging half his mum's washing line with him.

He stays frozen in the box and peers out through the slit at the now silent door hole.

If he moves a muscle will it just come plunging and howling back in? He would rather be somewhere else, but this is on balance so much better than it was a minute back that his instincts tell him to make no moves or changes straight away.

Jan Gordon shuts the whining hound in her utility room saying,

"You stay there Biff, and don't start howling again if I find a cat in the shed and bring him in for some milk... okay"

She heads back down the garden; she knows it could just be a squirrel or a rabbit, but if it was a cat, wonders if it will have sneaked out the shed and be already gone.

As she nears the little shed she starts to say,

"It's okay little cat if you're still there, you can come out now Biff is shut indoors.

She reaches the door and fiddles to release the padlock.

Bobcat crouched and ready to do battle sees the light of day flood in. Still peering through the gaps in the fruit box he cannot think why, yet is pleased no hound rushes through.

A kindly looking lady gazes down on him and calls a fond hello but does not rush to him. She knows a frightened cat just cannot help being ferocious when it thinks it's cornered.

Instead she makes those kissing sounds and a selection of words with those encouraging high tones that take her voice as far as possible from anything like a growl.

She walks a short way off saying,

"come on little cat, there's milk and food up at the house if you are hungry… or else you're just free to go and I can lock the shed again and let Biff back out."

Although none of those words mean a thing to Bob he knows the tone is from some kind of friend. He stands up and hops out of the box. Now out he sees the woman crouch with arm outstretched as Annie often does when she wants to pick him up and cuddle him. His feet are walking towards her while his brain is still putting things in cat order.

A warm hand strokes his head and tickles his chin, then a surprised tone,

"oh you're a Manx… well then hello little Manxy, or is there a collar with your name on it? No… then Manxy you will have to be!"

Bob feels this sort of touch and voice could come from people who open tins of food and have warm cushions by their fire. When someone strokes your head like this they do not suddenly strike out at you or feed you to their hound. His instincts say that he can trust this human.

Now she stands and walks towards the house a few steps.

"Are you coming with me little Manxy; I've got milk and bickies, or some of Biff's meat… it's okay, when we get inside he will just think that you might be our old Rusty come back from the dead!"

Bobcat follows and feels there's something 'mum'ish' about this lady and he feels a meow come out; she stops and turns with,

"Blimey Manxy, that sounded more like a Siamese yowl… ah yes, I see your long nose now. Well we are honoured to have you as a guest. Have you walked all the way from Siam today?"

Then she comes a few steps back and picks him up, and Bob enjoys the heat and smell of her.

In what remains of her garden and the path up to the house he only vaguely thinks that the hound might be inside, and anyway he somehow knows that she is in control of what will happen there.

She holds him up under her chin to give herself one free hand to open the back door, and in they go.

Bobcat flinches and recoils rather at the suddenly renewed scent of bloodhound but from high up here and no appearance of the dog itself things seem okay.

Mrs Gordon puts him down on the floor and he crouches a little nervously. The sound of cupboard doors and tins give creak and bang and phut and wind to click and twang… and smell of meat and jelly curls the air.

Bloodhound gives a rising moan beyond his door yet Bobcat knows it's not for him this time.

The lady comes away from her work-surface with two bowls of food, though one has much more in it than the other. She puts the big one down on a plastic mat beyond the fridge, and the small one on the floor quite near the door.

"Come on Manxy, this is yours here… don't go near that other one or you'll end up as a dinner yourself!"

Bobcat tucks hungrily into his bowl and hears his lady walk across to the side door into the utility room and continues munching.

A jangle of a collar and skidding of blunt clawed feet on the tiles makes him glance round and he freezes in horror at the sight of an enormous hound loping in to devour his equally enormous breakfast.

Bobcat rises on his toes, and his fur rises on his back; even his breakfast rises in his throat but he swallows hard as he gulps in horror.

For the moment he seems safe because the bloodhound seems intent on killing his bowl of meat, and the nice lady is back in with them. Only when he gets two thirds of the way through his bowl does he glance up. His chomp chomp chomp stops abruptly, and his huge ears lift like tent flaps while he looks across at Bobcat who with growing confidence had gone back to his breakfast. Does the dog wonder if it's his old friend Rusty the cat suddenly alive again, we cannot tell; he is certainly not a bright dog, let's just hope he's not still a hungry dog!

Mrs Gordon is making herself a cup of real coffee and hanging around until both animals have finished their food. She wants to have a sit down in her lounge with her coffee and she would like to see if their visitor will come and join Biff in front of the fire.

Bobcat's bowl is clean and Biff's now also.

The lady walks a few steps and gesturing that way with her head and words like 'fire' and 'snooze' and 'you'll be alright

Manxy'; none of those words meant anything to Bobcat but her tone was reassuring.

As Bobcat sat undecided on the mat by the door Biff came a few steps forward made a low yelp and turned towards the lounge. Bobcat moves his head around to try and make his thoughts fall into place, then follows this big dog into the huge front room.

"Come over by the fire Manxy... it's okay I can tell that Biff has decided he likes you."

Bobcat has heard 'Manxy' often enough now to realise that it links him to certain possibilities. Each time he hears it there will be something he can have or do, so his job is just to work out what's being offered to him.

Here now everything seems to suggest... well, at least if you see how everyone has moved in on and found a place near the fire, things seem to suggest to Bob that both the dog and the lady want him to share their warmth.

He pads nervously forward and the dog who was sitting up and watching him puts his nose down on his paws with the same noise as when you let the last bit of air out of a balloon, or fart into a cushion!

Bobcat settles down on the rug.

The dog even shuffles a little way towards him.

Mrs Gordon is tickled at the thought of her Biff having a friend again, because he won't allow another dog into the house... so seeing him now she sits back with her mug of coffee and smiles a contented smile.

Chapter Seven

Her Dreams Travel West

She is getting ready for bed, but like any decent kid spinning it out as long as she can.

Half of her would quite like to sink into a dream and sail away to see where Bobcat has got to; she is also fairly eager to stay up and watch the next programme, because her mum says it would be unsuitable and that there are too many naughty bits keep happening in it!

Annie protests to her mum that she likes seeing people being naughty, any sort of naughty… and thinks to herself she would be happy to find it is the kind of naughty that people do without clothes because she is particularly keen to learn more about how that sort of naughty is done!

Secretly she knows partly what sort of naughty it is because last week back at the old house after a tip off from one of her classmates that there were 'good bits' in it, she had crept back down the stairs after she had been told by her friend to listen out from upstairs for the breathy saxophones to start playing low and moodily.

That night from the darkened hallway where the sitting room door is always left ajar so her mum can hear up the stairs, Annie had peeped through at some people on telly getting ready for bed; then before they had put their pyjamas on, starting a sort of slow motion wrestling match but with a lot of kissing… and not only on the mouth!

While the people on the telly were wrestling and kissing,

Mum and Dad also untucked each other's clothes as though they were getting ready to come up to bed, so Annie had felt it wise to sneak away back up the stairs.

So although she now knows it is naughty to do slow wrestling and kissing when you are supposed to be getting ready for bed, she cannot really see why it matters if she stays up to watch it, because there is nobody that she can wrestle with back upstairs even if she wanted to copy it.

Dee comes in with a mug of hot chocolate for her:

"Are you ready to go up to bed now Annie, that programme that you wouldn't like starts in fifteen or twenty minutes time, so it will be just about the right time for us to get you settled."

"Oh can't I stay down and watch it just this once Mum, it's not school tomorrow… please Mum?"

"No Annie because it would frighten you and give you nightmares; it's really not the sort of thing you like."

"But I'm not frightened of people wrestling when they go to bed Mum!"

"Hey… but what makes you think they wrestle Annie?"

"I was coming downstairs to get a drink at our old house, I know it's when the music goes all slow and wheezy and it's their time for bed. But instead of going straight to sleep they are naughty and they start sort of slow wrestling before they have put their pyjamas on.

"But I wouldn't copy it anyway Mum, because there's nobody for me to wrestle with upstairs is there?"

Dee looks soberly into the fire and wonders what else Annie might have seen. She gives her girl a hug and a kiss, and asks her if she thinks Bobcat might have come home again when they wake up next morning.

Annie is a little quiet for a few moments. She is remembering where he was last night and the determined way he padded along the path and through the woods.

When he settled in his box of rags in the shed her dreams had drifted off to other things, like her friends in school and a trip they all took; how the school minibus bumped and bounced up a long drive between spreading lofty cedar trees, like the ones that were along the cinder drive that leads to the house in the courtyard they have just moved away from.

Annie's thoughts return:

"No I doubt it Mum; even if he has decided to come home he is too far away to be back tomorrow. Anyway Mum… he doesn't know the way back now. I don't think he knows where this new house is, he only knows the old house in the courtyard; I think it might be where he is going."

"Ah well maybe love… shall we go upstairs now?"

"Okay Mum, I feel quite sleepy now…"

While Dee goes down to watch the bedtime wrestlers without pyjamas, Annie sinks through crimson gloom to darkness. In her dream she is flying over moors, and far below the granite rocks glow luminous and green.

She can see a young gardener who walked and worked and scrounged, and a couple of times even stole on his way from Kent to Cornwall; now he has a home and a job at a big house on the edge of a moor.

Young Jake Jones is very happy in his new life as gardener and handyman at this big house; and he's really good friends with the other lad called Rick who works there too.

This is all a long time in the past, the year is 1913 and next year after this one a terrible war will start in Europe, and a retired brigadier from the Boer war will begin encouraging and cajoling all the local lads to join the army.

Annie can see him with his mates from the village all getting on their bikes to cycle into their nearest town.

She sees the manly confident grins as they troop into the army recruitment office, and each eager to be the first to get their name down and be rewarded with the King's shilling.

Then back out into the sunlight they swagger to wink laddishly at the admiring cluster of girls who greet them, and who the lads now have money to buy a drink for and receive kisses and other favours from. So they gesture them to follow across to the pub… and stragglers who haven't joined up yet, stare shamefacedly, and decide they might soon get some of this fun and admiration for themselves.

Annie dreams that she is now there with this group of girls. One turns to her and speaks:

"Hi Annie… yes, you coming over too? You can have a glass of beer as well, as long as you kiss them all and let them squeeze you and stuff."

Annie suddenly feels so grown up and knows she has somehow has passed beyond the half grown girl she was. She girlishly links arms with the lass who had spoken to her and they cross the road.

In the smoky glass clinked twilight of The Masons Arms, it is like Annie has entered a new world, and she is not as much shorter than the grown-ups as she thought she was. She can feel that she has now moved into the body of a young woman, though in her head she is just the same.

With the outbreak of war it is like a carnival in the town, and girls and women who would rarely venture near the pubs now laugh and chat inside.

She is taking in all this sound and movement when she is almost lifted off her feet by a strong young man who whirls her round to face him:

"Hello pretty lady, can I buy you a drink… but first is there a kiss and your blessing for a soldier who will soon be on his way to the war."

Annie smiles her best and sweetest smile and raises on tip-toes to be able to kiss him. Her eager but by any stranger un-kissed lips meet his warm lips and she does a nice hmmwa while she delivers a real smacker; she is finished, but is still held against his mouth as though it were not done. Annie thinks perhaps she did it a bit fast and starts again but slowly this time… and he turns his head on one side and Annie feels her lips being parted rather… which she cannot remember her mum ever doing!

Finishing he takes a big breath and says,

"So what's your drink going to be little lady?"

"Oh a glass of beer please."

"Which one do you like miss?"

"Oh hum, just the usual beer please"

To Annie beer is beer is beer, what's all this about which one would she like; she nearly asks him which one is the most grown up, but stops herself.

He gets her half a pint of mild and brings it to her. Annie thanks him sweetly, and feeling all geed up and womanly at having completed her kissing test, turns to go and talk to the girl that as they all crossed the road she had linked arms with. As she arrives the more worldly-wise girl who had been watching her progress says quickly:

"No Annie you can't come straight over here; when you accept a drink off a boy you have to talk with him for at least… well, as long as he wants to talk, or until he goes off to his mates… he may even want to squeeze you or something."

Annie, with the realisation that there is still much to learn in this new procedure, asks the girl if she has ever done all this before.

"Of course Annie… each Saturday morning there will be a few lads come to sign up from a village across the moor, or farm somewhere. There is always a group of us hanging around near the recruitment office to cheer them, and afterwards they can't wait to spend some of their King's shilling in the pub and be kissed by lots of girls."

Annie starts to cotton on to the rules and goes straight back and as though making amends for her behaviour she reaches up and kisses him on the cheek and smiles sweetly and asks his name.

"I'm Richard… or Rick; I work at a big house across the moor with Jake over there."

Annie scans all the faces beyond the corner of the bar; she can see one or two of the boys she feels she knows vaguely from school and senses there is some confusion here; she is not quite certain where Rick was trying to point, then spotting the boy, she feels she has seen him earlier in her mind's eye and she says,

"Is Jake that handsome one with the very tanned skin Rick?"

"Well I wouldn't call him handsome as such, but he's fairly tanned because he came mostly on foot all the way from Kent not that long ago."

"Oh that's funny Rick I live in Ken… yes, in Kent."

Now Annie feels a little strange, and distance starts to shape her life, and time and other closes round these passing moments.

Now where she is has moved or changed, or is it she that has moved or changed… and seeing gone the rocks and moorland wastes, now down below are fields and towns and farms with old oast houses.

Annie's dreaming eye is searching through the shapes and colours of her sleeping mind for her little cat, and searching for the little shed that she knows he spent last night in. Finding it she is drawn to the house where even now the door is opening into the garden, and from which emerge a large hound, a small woman and indeed, a little cat.

The dog lopes quickly to a ball and picks it, then offers it to the cat who knows it's intended as a gift to stop and play with but he has set his mind on going; going on along his way to… where?

Bobcat only knows to go, and to keep going and keep looking, to find the thing that's missing in his world. He can still feel the memory of those colours and sounds and smells that he only knows are somewhere out there… So he goes.

Biff goes with him down the lawn and through the pine trees past the shed.

Mrs Gordon wasn't sure if Manxy just wanted to go outside for the toilet or for something else. She can tell by the way that Biff is padding along with him that her dog knows there is a voice in the wind that is calling the little cat.

Right down at the bottom there is the hole in the wooden fence. Bobcat glances and smiles sideways at the hound and goes straight through. He is down the bank and back onto the path as he hears behind him a mournful howling wail coming over the fence.

Biff knows he has gone, then hears;

"Come on Biff old boy, fetch your ball back and I'll throw it for you."

He turns reluctantly to face his dear mum.

"Oh you poor old chap you look so sad, but he may call in again some day."

Mrs Gordon turns toward the house knowing Biff may well wait beside the hole a while; and thinking also, that as he will not let another dog in the house, perhaps next time she hears of somebody with a litter of kittens needing homes she will get one as a friend for Biff.

Chapter Eight

Woods and Railway Lines

Four black feet pad with purpose along the riverbank, though the path itself now curves away from water and into the splashed filtered light of jagged ash trees.

Bobcat sees the path diverging but leaves it to stay with the river.

Why does he stay with the river? Certainly he is going to want a drink now and then but it seems to be for something else that he opts to go this way.

The distant glowing rose of the sky is shrinking and darkening like the final night sealed bud of summer.

He sees in his mind the memory of a time when if he was out at the end of day, perhaps deep in the wood beyond the garden; as he wandered back to be with his people and their fire and his food, there was often a sky just like this high and beyond the courtyard flats and stables. Stables where long before Bobcat, around eighty years earlier Jake Jones had lived above in the loft when he worked there as a young gardener.

Bobcat's thought process tells him that he must always at this time of day walk towards the rosy sky and by this he will sooner or later walk back through the archway and into the big cobbled courtyard and his real home.

The trouble is that a cat does not have the logic to see that even if by some fluke he does end up in the right place, his people have gone to live somewhere else. Though he was there in the new house with them for a little while himself, he was not there long enough… it was too temporary to have been established in his memory as home.

So Bobcat pads along the river bank, and bright yellow celandines and sombre pink wood sorrel glow sleepily on the night banked green; and further where the riverbank slopes to a chalky bay for the burbling stream, a procession of dreaming primrose nod the sheeny grey roots of beech along, where also tiny field mouse scuttles eagerly from hole then squeaks too loudly in this settling dark.

In the short frantic life of a little mouse, you don't see many cats out here, but here's one crouched a moment till he springs… then field mouse makes a nice hot tasty woodland 'take-away'.

Annie watches fondly through the serried layers of her dream, and thinks he seems to know his way… sees him padding off along his woodland route and can see he is a little animal content to make his life and take his chances where he goes.

She looks ahead further along the snaking river and the fragrant night soaked wood; the dying glow of the distant western sky still just kisses the star beckoning fingertips of the highest leaves, but does not filter down into the mole-tunnelled dark beneath.

Annie looks beyond a few miles on and there she sees, that there is a railway-line running across a grass and thorn banked ridge; and spanning a small valley in the middle of this great forest.

Her thoughts and dreams had been drifting away to other things and places, but seeing the railway ahead and thinking that if he keeps going and does not stop to rest or sleep her little cat will get there sometime through this night, knows she must try to keep herself in this region of her dreams.

His nimble silky feet pad on and the river leads him down this little valley.

He almost leaps into the river in shock when a huge pheasant panics and takes off with a frantic whirr of its wings from right beside his ear; had it just stayed crouched for another second he would have been past it and gone. It clatters up through the hazel saplings and a few feathers flutter back down, then it sails away down the valley calling 'chucuk chucuk, chucuk chucuck, and so on and so forth until it's gone.

Yet here now is a problem; his instincts tell him to stick with the river until… well, until his instincts tell him to do something else, so on finding a steep climbing wall of stringy grass and youthful saplings that his river has gone into a dark hole through, what should he do?

He peers into the dark and there is no path; both walls are slimy brick and go right down to the wet bit. 'Mouldy mice' he thinks… well, probably something a bit like it. He wants to stay with the river but not so much that he is prepared to jump in and swim through.

For the first time in quite a while he sits down on his bony little tail-less bum, but a thistle makes him rise again. He pads a few paces forward and sniffs and scrutinizes the ground before he commits his un-padded bum to having to sit.

After a few moments of seated thought he is padding around the leafy woodland floor to help him choose his route; the sounds of this wood at night float past him; first the 'shim shim shim' from a fallen rotting birch tree where a large brown cricket calls out to find himself at bit of romance; next the irritated voice of some disgruntled blackbird that has been driven from the comfy perch it thought it had got for the night… Then sudden and absolute, the unmistakeable song of the nightingale:

'There could be no mistaking the nightingale even if heard for the first time,

A super musician of a heavenly state,

Every bird note thrilled the air, and notes that seemed could not come from earthly living creature;

I stopped abruptly at the first note heard.'

Bobcat stops abruptly at the first note he hears. He stops, but not so as better to hear its wondrous song, but just to see if it is somewhere near enough for him to turn it into food. It sits in a tangle of thorn bushes a short way off and sings up at 'the yellow sickle of the new moon' that is 'just riding above the hazel hedge, with 'even its pale light dimming the stars about it.' Seeing Bobcat loitering with nose upturned the nightingale opts to swap to the rotten branch of a big old beech tree some way off, from where its song returns as a bright cascade of ice crystals.

From where its song returns, as a bright cascade of ice crystals;

With his field mouse not digested yet he is definitely not hungry enough or desperate enough to leap into a thorn bush and clamber up through sharp prickles in an undoubtedly futile attempt to catch the nightingale… so just to get a good view as it flies away! So there is some relief that it has gone.

With or without a second course to his meal he has at least digested all the sounds of the night, and seems to have settled upon the route that he will take.

Bobcat sidles slyly through several porcupine like yellow flowered bushes of broom that sprout from a mound of sandstone and rubble that was brought here and dumped on the bank when railwaymen were doing some work on the line ten years ago.

Now Bobcat climbs this mound and sniffs the pungent scent of the broom as its green stems nod darkly and its yellow flowers glow.

Finding a gap and pushing beneath a rather tired looking railway fence of rusty wire mesh he starts the climb. He is halfway up the embankment when far far away he hears a distant hoot that might be an owl yet doesn't register in his little head as being that.

At the top of the grassy bank the world opens up to him and the starry sky is vast and dark and deep, and it goes and goes and goes… and goes away from you. But to a little cat it looks as if it could be just a few metres above his head… like Annie's bedroom ceiling at the last house, with all the luminous stars stuck across so when Dee put Annie's light out they would twinkle… well, at least glow down at her.

Though distant, Annie sees him now, and though she sleeps her dreaming thoughts are with him there.

What, he thinks, are these strange dark rails so long and straight with those two as shiny as mum's cat food fork, but this first one dark beside the others and standing high. Being a cat, and drawn to be up on anything that gives you a better view Bobcat takes a skip and a jump and is sitting up on the cold black rail.

The cold does not worry him, and the view ahead is quite a revelation, but there is a distinctly strange tingling in the pads of his feet.

There is the merest hint of a faint mist tickling the bracken and foxgloves that tangle here and there along the side of the railway. All the metal rails are wet with beads of dew, and as well as the tingle he feels through his feet his whiskers detect a faint but sparky sizzling in the air around him.

He is content for now to sit on his high viewing perch and gaze on down the valley to where the forest finishes and fields resume; though the waves of electrical charge that skim up and down the fur on his back are a little annoying. If he knew he was sitting on enough electrical voltage to fry him and launch him into space like a shooting star if any part of his body touches the ground… he would not be sitting so content.

Again he can be glad he has no tail, for if he had, and by now he is relaxed enough to let it droop behind him to the stony floor, Well then his big adventure would finished right now.

The strange owl hoots through the wood and nearer now, with its hoots half masked by a rattled train-like echo somewhere through the trees. Bobcat's ears twitch and twist as though he seeks to hear its muffled flapping wings and spot its swooping path before it spots him.

His level of concern is minimal, for not only is he not owl's sort of food, it doesn't sound much like the fur tingling screech of the big white rather scary barn owl who haunts the gardens round the courtyard where Bobcat thinks he lives.

An occasional ear twitch is quite adequate to keep up to speed on what's around when you feel as in control as he does just now.

So now why does his high rail seem to quiver as he sits, and almost feel to rumble as he goes from crouched to upright sensing time or life is moving through this wood.

If time is moving, then he feels perhaps it's time to move.

Hunching forward he would reach carefully down to step away from his rumbling perch… then a voice in his head,

"Bobby no, don't step down, just jump, and keep jumping till you're across the lines and down the other side."

His rumbling perch becomes a howling roar and lights of a train flare round the bend, and hack towards a small black furry ball of disbelieving fright.

With leap and bound he clears the rails and then the next and tall one goes below and down the bank he flails and the 2.10 night mail train from London clatters through.

Chapter Nine

Breakfast

A chiselling pecker drums on wood to tell prospective mates he's opening up shop ready for this season to begin... well, he drums as you would too were you a woodpecker!

A blackbird searching out his breakfast grubs and worms along the edge of the field sees an unwelcome visitor sound asleep beneath the hedge and jumps and flutters up into low branches where it throws down a ping ping ping of aggravated rebukes. One of Bobcat's ears wakes up and twist with irritation at the noise; without opening an eye he measures the distance to this unwelcome songster that he might all things being equal turn into a very welcome breakfast.

The noisy feathered breakfast sounds close enough to be worth him opening an eye.

One black eye half opens... slowly... the hot breakfast carries on shouting down its flurry of heated objection, and at which the cat remembers that these sorts of meal sometimes get so obsessed with shouting at you that they keep hopping closer and closer from twig to twig, and as you finally pounce it is as easy as stealing and eating a couple of grapes in a supermarket; not that our cat has ever stolen grapes in a supermarket but I expect you have.

The sneaky open black eye stays half open with its dark middle bit huge so you cannot see the yellow round the outside, and you can hardly tell it isn't shut.

If Bobcat had a tail it would be hard to stop it switching from side to side in eager anticipation which might have had the effect of alerting the bird, so this is yet another advantage of not having a tail. The only disadvantage here will be if he does leap and try to run up along the branch that droops almost to the ground. Cats who do have tails, tails' give him or her instant information whether they are tipping off one side or not as they run and balance.

So Bobcat waits, and waiting, probably cannot calculate the chances of succeeding with his sprint up the branch... no that's not really true; he can calculate in the cat sense... cats have spent millions of years on this planet refining their ability to calculate the odds and so to pick their best chance of a meal without burning fruitless energy.

As he looks up the branch at the scolding blackbird he does not come up with a figure of say... twenty or forty or sixty percent chance of grabbing first prize, but his brain computes almost perfectly whether he is likely to succeed, or fairly certain to succeed, or if there is no chance whatsoever.

It's a tricky one this, but he knows he can pull it off, especially if the stupid bird panics and tries to fly the way it's facing which is straight towards the cat's mouth! And he has caught quite a few like that before. But there is enough doubt to make him continue the waiting game; perhaps the obliging bird will be really helpful and hop all the way to the end of the bow and allow itself to be plucked like some nice ripe apple from a summer orchard.

Rustle rustle and an excited squeak sizzles eagerly from the bank below the hedge. Bobcat's mental computer switches from the reasonable possibility of a stupid but proximity-aware blackbird, to the absolute certainty of a plump corn fed and very dim field vole.

Seeing the cat sitting suddenly straight up the bird emits a startled shriek and takes off straight over Bobcat's head who was about to ignore it and go for this vole on the bank. He finds he has leapt up and caught it in mid flap and touches down again with breakfast already on the table. A few deep crunches stop the squawking… now what about that nice fat vole?

"Do you know somewhere around here where a railway line goes through the middle of a wood Mum?"

Annie and Dee are walking to school and their feet go flap flap fl fl flap flappapap as Annie's shorter legs synchronise with then dislocate their step from Dee's longer strides.

'Cars and men on foot from drives and gateways leave to go their way,

And settle on the bigger roads where many seethe like ants or wash in droves towards the town.

And all around, the sense of something new is in the air, though all did this the day before, and all will do the same again…

But all set off like something new is in the air.'

"Why do you need a railway line in a wood Annie, is it some sort of project at school?"

"No I don't need one Mum, I just need to know where there is one round here. You see that's where Bobby is… at least where he was last night.

"He's okay now, but he only just got across the railway line as the train was coming. I had to shout at him not to touch any of the rails because he can't tell which ones' carry electricity... well of course he doesn't even know what electricity is either.

"But he did make it across, I watched him run down the bank the other side... oh yes Mum, and there's a field just beyond the wood there... so can you think where it is then Mum?"

"I haven't got the faintest idea love, Kent must have at least two thousand woods where a railway runs through the middle."

"Except with this one there's a field just beyond the railway line Mum!"

"Yes Annie, and of those two thousand about five hundred have also got a field along the edge or wherever it was love!"

"So are you quite sure you don't know the one I'm talking about Mum?"

"Well no Annie..."

It's funny how children always believe that grown-ups know everything and have been everywhere.

Dee looks fondly down at her imaginative daughter. She knows her girl has unique strengths and talents, but to believe that her revelations each morning can not be simply a hangover from her night's dreaming will only happen when some proof floats into their life.

Their big and little feet tap on along the road, and friends call 'hi' across the street.

Annie waves and calls back, then she becomes reabsorbed in thought.

'She sniffs the morning air, her dreaming starts, she is walking down a dusty Kentish lane in quiet September, slowly night departs… where will Bob be tonight when she searches through her dreams again?'

Chapter Ten

Lucky for One

When he looked out from beneath the hedge on the bank where he'd slept that night, he could see right over to the other side of the enormous field that lay in front.

Not quite with horror at the prospect, but certainly some trepidation he gazed out over it, like he was a shipwrecked mariner standing on the bewildering shore of an ocean that would have to be crossed.

He could see that beyond its far side it fell into another shallow valley, but that in it there were trees quite tall enough to poke their leafy heads above the parapet.

Now time has passed, and the little cat has set sail in his ship of hope across, and with the tallness of the grass around him the far side of the field is no longer visible.

He will be able to keep going in the right direction; he will not know how he is doing it though it is fairly simple, for even a simple creature to do. The sun is climbing in the south eastern sky, and he will just keep it behind and to his left.

A skylark climbs on its ladder of song, up and up through the high sweet air, and trilling as though it were scattering its own piano sonata along the lifting breeze. Now she changes and retunes her melody; it sounds as if she knew and were trying to paraphrase the fluttering notes of a delicate Chopin sonata.

Bobcat pads along but hearing music overhead glances up at this singing lark-burger to ascertain the possibilities for an early lunch… she halts her dulcet tones and glances down to see that where he is going will not give him the chance to turn her nest of babies into his next meal!

She can see that if he maintains his present course and direction he will soon be past her nest and beyond.

This day seems settled fair, and a mild breeze wafts steadily over this field of flowing grasses.

These passages with clear goals and direction would be a pleasant time of simple voyage if you could switch off all niggling anxiety. A cat is never completely at ease in the middle of nowhere; they prefer to be where they can see one or two escape routes to take if things suddenly get tricky.

Time ticks, or slides perhaps, and fairly nonchalantly as Bob crosses the vastness of the hay field. Even just the grass is way above his head, except where it is laid by wind and rain; then here and there are thistles and taller weeds that stand like trees in the jungle of grass.

It does not arrive as music to his ears… Bobcat is trundling along at a pretty good speed for a cat, and is pretty much halfway across the field and pushing through a rather weedy patch. Therefore it does not arrive as music to his ears, and is certainly not a welcome arrival when the distant but distinct barking of two dogs reaches him from away in the echoing woods to his right.

They are a fair way off and might just as easily be barking at some squirrel safe up a tree. Bobcat wishes he were also safe up a tree rather than pushing to make good speed through this wilderness of herb and grass.

His ancient instincts tell him that the sound is moving, that they are down wind and might have picked up his scent.

As if suddenly startled he jumps forward and starts to run. The two howling dogs sound like they have found stronger scent and are in for the kill, and their bark has lost its echo meaning they are out of the woods now and into the field.

Bobcat has never done this before… not this being chased in the wild by two murderous dogs, and unless he is very lucky may not live to do this again. The only two things that balance the odds are that because he is small and dark and the grass is tall they are chasing his scent not yet seeing his desperate form; and because they are chasing his scent while he is running across the wind they are still running towards where he was a few seconds earlier when he is in fact further on.

Yet the big curve they are running will reach him unless he gets to safety first.

Bobcat's little heart is pumping at six times its normal speed and his lungs are gasping air at the same speed as his legs are flailing back and forth.

Here comes the fence and the grass near the wood is shorter so he can get a bit of speed on, but he hears the pitch of the dogs voices change as they finally get a sight of him. Bob's through beneath the lowest strand of barbed wire and into the wood still running hard.

The first dog gets to the fence and goes at it full tilt, and he cuts his back up on a sharp wire barb but hardly knows.

As the dogs howl into the wood the trees echo with their baying and Bobcat's instincts aim him at a tree. A leap at trunk and frantic scrabble, and don't slip and fall back now Bobcat or you're a dogs' dinner.

Two Staffordshire bull terriers charge the final few metres and leap up at him, but he is safely on the first branch and way above their reach.

That would probably be that for now; like when dogs corner a squirrel up a tree that does not reach its branches across to other trees and the wee beastie has to stay put stuck there as he is, it never takes that long; pretty soon the dogs get bored and wander off.

Today what happens is that after ten or so minutes the calling voices of two approaching women catches Bobcat's ear. He lifts his eyes from the baying terriers who themselves glance round like naughty boys whose game is up and allow their howling to settle somewhat.

The women come over a stile some way to the right and a third dog on a lead is guided underneath then kept at heel.

Bobcat looks across and knows… Mrs Gordon and Biff and a female friend come scuffing through last years now sun crisped autumn leaves, and crunching twigs beneath their feet.

Biff is the first to know it's Bob; he looks up and lets out a baleful call as only a bloodhound can, and which makes his mum look down at him with confused surprise, then up into the tree where despite Biff's non-hunting moan she still expects to see a stranded squirrel.

"Aaah… so Manxy, what can you possibly be doing here my little friend?"

To which Bobcat fails to find an answer, but the woman's friend says,

"Must have been having a nice day out in the countryside Jan… oh I see what you've just said now, do you think this might be the same little cat you were telling me you looked after the other day?"

"Oh there is absolutely no question Mary, with that long nose and stumpy tail… yes and just look at old Biff sitting there with love in his eyes and nearly wetting himself."

"Well isn't that remarkable Jan, it's almost as if he's a cat on a journey somewhere. Is there anything you think we should do for him?"

"I suppose we might try to help him back down though no doubt he can manage, and I know Biff would love to have a chat with him again; but with your terriers here that would never work. I suppose there is nothing but to leave him to it."

Bobcat has still been throwing nervous glances at the two terriers, but when he looks down at the upturned face of Biff his eyes relax and narrow into a cat smile that Biff sees and understands.

The two women look up at Bob on his safe branch and Mary who is very tall can just reach high enough to tickle him under the chin. Then with a few 'good luck little Manxy' type words and other phrases they lead their dogs away to the wooden stile, and slowly back across the field to the wood they had emerged from.

As they are entering the wood again Jan Gordon stops and glances back. She can still just see her dog's little companion in the tree, and no doubt waiting till they're well away till he descends.

Jan wonders will she hear of him again in this life… and where will his travels take him; perhaps to finish on his own she asks, but hopes it will be with his folks again.

Bobcat does not sit up there on his branch watching them go, running through the do's and don'ts of the field he nearly didn't make it across, yet the next time on his journey that he emerges from a wood and sees there is a field in his way, something in his instincts might lead him round the edge of it.

Sporadic barking choruses from the distant wood whenever a squirrel is flushed and chased up a tree; but now its ringing echo is fading and shows they are deep into the wood and heading away.

Peace returns across the field and Bobcat sniffs the wind that has shaken, ventilated, then absorbed the breath of herbs and daisies and so carries their scent in its soft flow. It is a flow that often now carries the thermic gusts you find when the sun is at or near its zenith. He knows this feel in the air, is aware of the high light of the sun pushing shadows to their shortest; then they start to creep through the afternoon back towards long again. Bobcat hears also the little skylark still bravely singing in the high sweet air.

'And overhead the larks still bravely singing fly'

Standing rather stiffly up, Bob turns carefully round on his branch and with a final sniff and a scout around grabs the trunk and reverses back down the tree like a little bear.

It is rather unnerving being back down here again, but no howling hounds come crashing through the undergrowth. To get his bearings he looks all around then up to where the sun shimmers and winks through the murmuring fingers of a fresh leafed oak tree… he is on his way again.

'And overhead the Larks...'

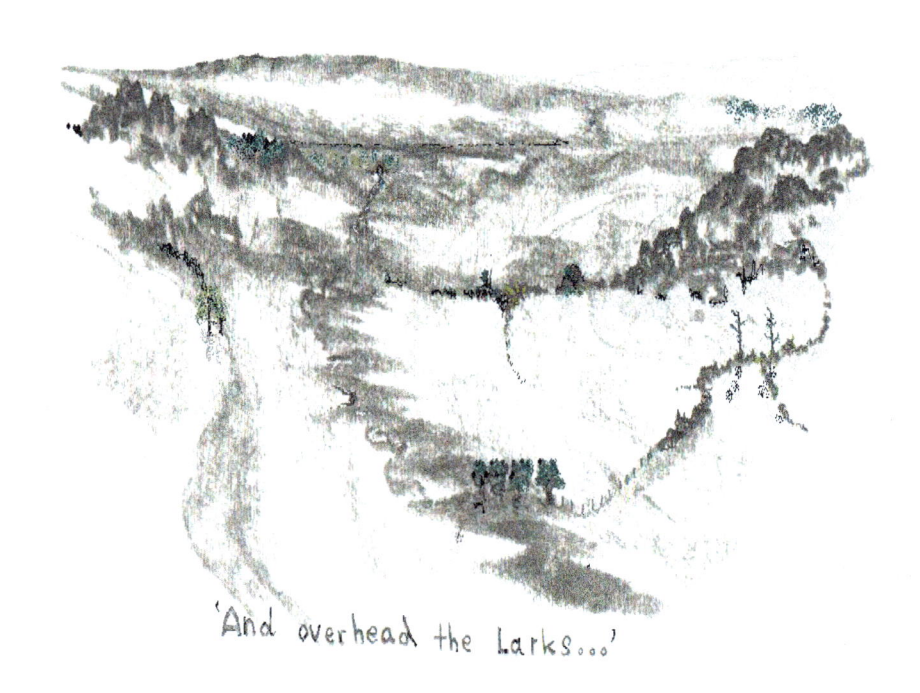

Note: Is there anyone who cannot see Bobcat in the foreground of 'and overhead the larks'... trotting nervously along just a little way above the s of larks...

(Though you may need a magnifying glass to spot the little blighter!)

Chapter Eleven

The Playground

"So where do you reckon he's going to be by tonight Annie?"

She's being quizzed by a couple of her friends at break-time... they throw questions in a tone that tries almost to show humorous doubt at the confident way Annie has described her cat's route so far, yet carefully stops short of making fun of her.

It probably stops short because the truth is that these two girls are both sort of fans of Annie Sparks... fans it appears with a lot of respect, but tempered also with a certain degree of fear.

This degree of fear comes not through being scared of being beaten up if they step out of line, nor because she has the means or inclination to make their lives unpleasant; what they fear is her uncanny insight of their minds and thoughts, and the fact that Annie Sparks seems to be frightened of nothing and nobody... old or young!

Her lack of fear is what makes them fans of Annie.

Georgina Digger is a bright attractive girl, a year above Annie and with a fair share of womanly development for her age. For at least two obvious reasons she is popular with boys, but perhaps more so because conversely she is quite young in mind and self-confidence.

Amanda Grisslethwaite is as black as your hat... well not really, unless your hat is only as black as a lovely warm mahogany colour! Mandy's mum is as black as a very very dark brown person, but her dad is a white Lancashire steel-worker who was made redundant and moved south to start again as a joiner and renovator, bodging up beams and doing carpentry and stuff in big old houses.

Amanda is quite tall and always wins races. She has elegant features among the tangle of beads and curls her mum likes to give her; but her face seems always to be wearing a startled expression, as if she is still shocked to find she is not really black and not really white... she looks a bit like Gracie Fields wearing too much fake tan, or an Asian or Caribbean soap star from Coronation Street.

Amanda Gristlethwaite... like Gracie fields with a fake tan!

Sometimes Mandy will do a Saturday morning working with her dad de-nailing old timbers or collecting and carrying out old laths to burn in the garden of the house that he is working on, while he rips the old ceilings and walls down inside.

Mandy loves doing all that… and loves the bit of cash he gives her when they stop off at a pub on the way home so he to have a beer. Even more though, she loves, as she did the other day at school, to hear about Annie giving a long kiss with her mouth open to some lad that went to fight in a war that finished… well, ages back before Annie was even born, so how does Annie tell it so real!

That's probably it I suppose; Mandy will listen to Annie because Annie tells her about things that her own young logic would say can never be… yet that still seem so real. How could a young girl like Annie describe an open mouthed kiss like that if she had never done it; and if she hasn't then what is her gift to make it seem so real?

The exchange continues:

"I don't know George, it really all depends if something slows him up with crossing that big field and everything."

Annie has given this answer to the question of Bobcat's whereabouts, as she looks with a fixed gaze across the hundreds of heads in the playground.

The other two girls stare with languid anticipation at her as she lets her eyes settle and focus beyond the distance. Though knowing her mind is out there somewhere very private and unique, they both search their own heads, and likewise across the playground to seek clues as to achieving this same gift of sight.

Their heads continue feeling disappointingly much the same; neither finds their mind's eye skimming away from Kent over the chalk downs of Wiltshire where Annie says she saw white horses cut in the turf slopes, or flying on over Dorset and Somerset's wooded valleys to reach Devon, or on to the moors of Cornwall.

No, both are still just the same George and Mandy and good at lots of things but mostly just at being girls… which they carry off as well as any do.

Two other girls and a smallish, rather pretty boy with brown curly hair approach across the playground, walking purposefully with almost the manner of being some sort of committee.

"Hello you lot, this is Harry that I was talking about… you know, the one who told me he had kissed his cousin's friend last weekend, and both with their mouths open!"

Harry is a popular lad at school though mainly with girls, these two, Janice and Les are just the tip of the iceberg. in fact sometimes boys think he is gay because of his popularity and the time he spends hanging around with girls, but he is grudgingly acknowledged as being handsome, and therefore most boys are prepared to think he might just be capitalising on this; he is certainly never bullied for it; and being a London kid earns him some respect as well.

Annie with an air of some importance and authority comes quickly back to Les:

"Yeah got you Les… what's the thing then, I mean didn't it work very well for them or something?"

"It was quite good wasn't it Harry?"

"Yeah, but it mostly is… you see I've been doing all this stuff for years, so it's not new to me really girls. Remember I was in a London school till last year; everybody does it all day long up there!"

"What really Harry, it must be such fun going to school in London."

The committee seems to think it has set the scene and reached its main agenda:

"Would you show us Annie…? I mean with Harry as the boy, not actually to us, ya'know, because people will call us les's if you do it on us."

Annie throws a quip:

"But one of you is a Les!"

"Alright Annie Sparks you wise-guy!"

Annie is fairly happy to enlighten Les and her friend; she likes the look of Harry, and enjoys the kudos of being asked to do something a bit cool in the playground.

Apparently there is some boy one or even both of them fancies who will be at a party they are off to tonight, and a fairly large portion of snogging is expected to be on the menu.

"Shall we show them Harry?"

Harry is a little wrong footed by the arrival of Annie's confident words. He thought he would have to sort of woo her or sweet talk her into the display, and that bit was going to be part of his whole cool act… but finds she is more or less going to 'take the kick-off' herself.

Then Annie remembers how the new army recruit in Cornwall had at the same time as he kissed her run his hand briefly over her front:

"But only mouths Harry, no hands. Well hands are okay to stop us crashing or banging our heads… but you know what I mean!"

The other girls are quite bemused by Annie's demand, but assume Harry is in the know; but Harry is unsure though hides the fact; he feels that being so cool he should know this 'no hands' thing, so wracks his brains for what it could be.

Annie thinks regarding 'hands' that when she travelled in her dream she was not as she in truth is now, being physically more mature in Cornwall, more a young woman. Now in the real world she is still flat as an ironing board and it would just be embarrassing; like having him trying to scrump apples off someone's apple tree in winter!

Harry nods, and gestures with a sidelong jerked thumb displaying worldly experience,

"So no hands then… yeah that's cool Annie."

And runs a couple more possibilities through his head to think what 'no hands' means.

Each steps forward in the sunlit playground.

Both already have their lips prepared and semi puckered, and partially ajar as heads, one to north and one to south tilt skilfully to facilitate docking.

The kind old sun winks knowingly in the heavens.

You might almost believe in seeing their poise that they are about to waltz away across the playground.

Wide mouthed like two young blue whales trawling the ocean for plankton they collide quite slowly and softly. All are fascinated to see that two mouths which ought by adolescent rights to be shouting playground insults at the other, are apparently now fused in some form of non violent, non verbally aggressive... tasting perhaps, or at any rate some radical thing where strangely one is not pushing the other away; and the throats of both move rhythmic and deliberate as do babies' gulping milk.

Georgina wonders if when they come apart some gruesome squirmy thing will emerge born like a creature of lust from the depths of she or he, or even both... She is rather in awe of what life and her duty as a girl will call on her to perform at this party; apparently snogging is not terribly pleasant she observes, for both Harry and Annie keep their eyes closed, and a sort of pained scowl wrinkles the brow of each.

There is no real sound coming from them except a kind of stage whispered 'hm hmm'.

The audience were expecting some kind of running commentary or technical description, and feel a bit embarrassed in the silence, but of course both the instructors have got their mouths full right now; this feels more like a demonstration for deaf people, but they are all scared to discuss the demonstration while it is still in progress.

With a few uncertain jerks they have finished. Each stands back as though they had just then lit a firework... or that one of them has just farted, but licking their lips, swallowing, and grinning self-consciously.

"So was that okay Les...? I mean could you get the hang of how it goes from watching us. The best thing now is for you both to do it with Harry while I am here to steer you a bit and tell you in your ear what to do... and what not to do of course, like don't bite his tongue and stuff!"

The girls stare a little wide-eyed and aghast at all this; from the outside it all starts to look like one of those painful African tribal rituals that youngsters are put through as initiation into the adult world.

Les and her friend consider the merits of Annie's suggestion while the other girl (Janice) steps forward lips akimbo and Harry gulps a quick breath and braces himself.

Georgina sees Les step sideways looking a little less than keen to take her turn and fasten on to Harry's much-vaunted kisser. She ponders rather cruelly whether the 'Les by name and les by nature' bit may hold some truth!

As Janice is coached and after some moments told in her ear by Annie that it is probably long enough, she un-sticks and Harry takes a welcome break for air before Les grabs her turn with the best of them, and her sexual orientation ceases to be in any kind of doubt.

Les has successfully retrieved her tongue, and pulls apart having really taken quite a pride in what she was just doing. Annie turns to Mandy and George:

"What about you two having a crack at it while we've got Harry here to practice on?"

The Annie fan club starts to pucker up and close in, but Harry though with no malice intended comes quickly back with:

"Well okay that would be great, but perhaps another day for George and Mandy, I feel pretty shagged out after the first couple."

Harry's fire eating lips are no longer for hire, and the kissing circus leaves town.

Chapter Twelve

Two Weeks Later

Annie is walking home from School on Friday afternoon.

She and her friend amble along the hopscotch of higgledy pavement slabs down the long road that cuts like a knife through butter across one side of town.

Cars and lorries swish or rumble each way, and always fast along this straight; but as it is not a road that needs to be crossed her mum lets her come back down on her own most days… as long as it's with friends.

When they reach the road that forks left back up into the housing estate there is a small rec with swings and slides and seats. Dee will sit here waiting with her walkman pouring music into her ears, unless she's feeling cultured… then she'll have it tuned to Radio Four.

Halfway down the long hill Catherine stops going on about the girl who she reckons keeps trying to tempt her thought to be boyfriend away. It is as if she suddenly realises she has banged on about nothing else but her and him since they left class.

Cat shakes her head to reorient her thoughts, and takes a sudden breath as if waking herself up or re-focussing:

"So what of your cat…?"

"My Bobcat?"

"Yea that's it, Bobcat; you haven't said much for some days now Annie, do you still see him sometimes… you know, at night when you're asleep? Yes and thinking about it, I was talking to Alice about your cat yesterday and she asked me if you had been away trying to find the places where you think you have seen him at night."

"Yes, I have seen him quite a bit Cat, but it's been quite hard to find him sometimes. And also yes, I have tried to get Dad to take me looking for the places where I've seen him; he took me once but I couldn't describe properly what we had to look for, and we sort of drove around in circles and it seemed a bit pointless. It's only when you are looking for something the size of Bobcat that you realise how big everywhere is."

"Hey I've just thought Annie… when you find him in your dream, just look for the nearest street name and tell your dad in the morning!"

"Yeah I know, that's what Mum has said I should do, but in the dream I cannot seem to control things or remember what to do."

The girls amble on down the street with their thoughts and words. Cat wonders if she might recognise any of the places Bobcat has been and asks about the look of things.

A fair way down the hill Cat sights a socking great dog turd just ahead, and they both do a hop-scotch dance down the higgledy slabs towards it with their eyes closed (well almost) to play Russian roulette.

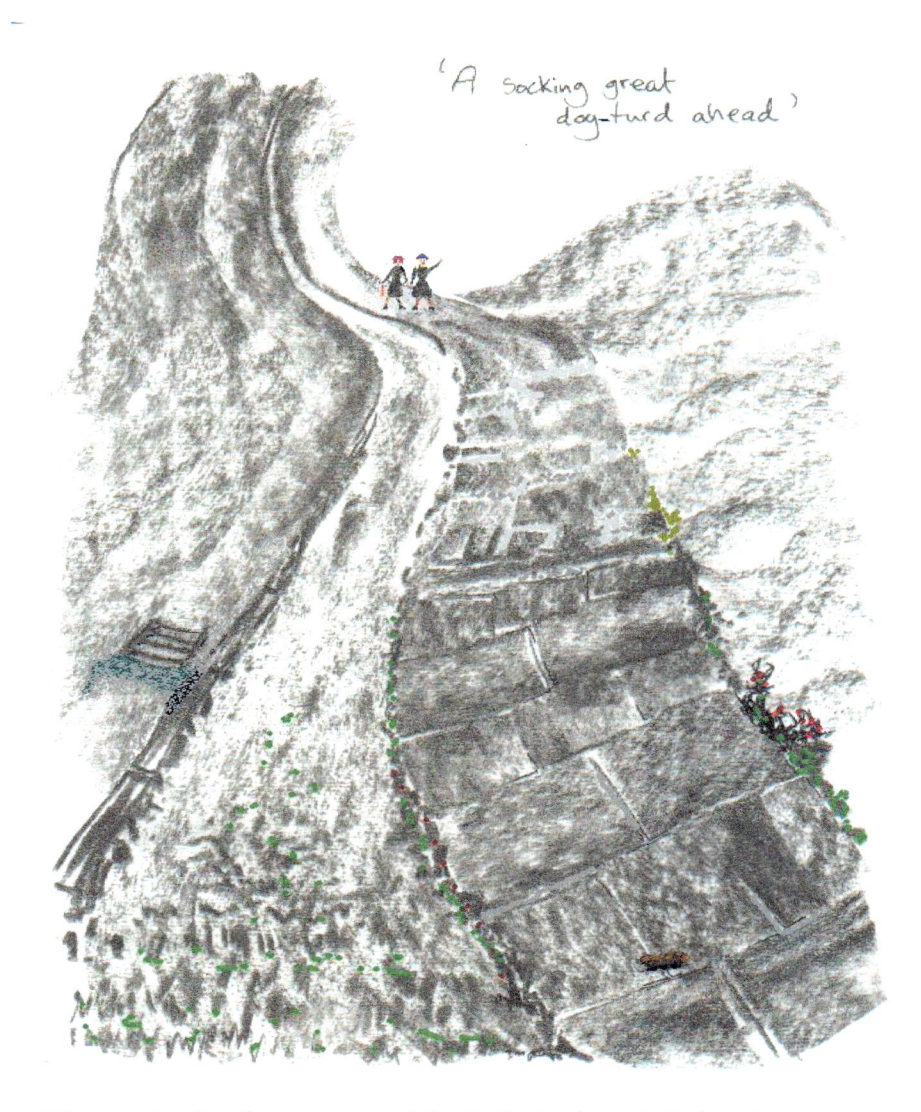

'A socking great dog-turd ahead'

They miss it of course, and halt their dog-shit-fandango to turn and look back at it… and as if all this were quite normal Annie continues with:

"The other night Bobcat was crossing one end of what looked like a big council estate; I think there were swings, but then there always are aren't there Cat? It might be different if I was able to say that there was a row of four swings and there were three yellow seats and the fourth one had a red seat!

"… He kept getting to gardens with a loose dog or a possessive tom-cat who would chase him back the other way. Or he would shelter from rain, and as it gets dark sleep in someone's garden shed and in the morning when he's still a bit dopey he takes ages to work out his direction properly."

"How do you know that Annie?"

"Well, 'cos when I look for him the next night and search on miles ahead where I expect him to be, he's nowhere to be seen; when the dream does find him he is only about three gardens on from where he was the night before!"

"So is he off that estate now?"

"Well he might be now, but he wasn't last night; there's a final road that runs down to the fields beyond the estate, I suppose you would call it a close, or a cul-de-sac Cat. Right at the end are some old council houses with a lot of old folks living there. As he was going past and I think he had just got the smell of the fields beyond there was some nice sweet little old lady putting milk bottles outside her kitchen door before she went to bed. She saw Bobby coming across her lawn and called him in."

"So what happened then?"

"No idea Cat, except that I saw he answered to her voice and went inside, I expect she found him a tin of sardines or something for his tea; my Bobcat could charm food out of the Devil himself! Then as often happens Cat, I think I went into deeper sleep, and my attention in the dream looses its focus and drifts away."

"When that happens Annie… em, does it make you feel like you are losing him, I mean like you've suddenly got to fight to stay with him?"

They come to a halt in the shade of an old lilac tree. Annie looks suddenly removed from here, or uncertain for a few moments, as if she has had to go somewhere to find the answer; when she looks up to answer Catherine you can see that the right thoughts and words are still just taking shape and forming in her mind.

"Yes, I suppose you would expect it to be really horrible seeing something you love so much just fading from your sight and reach… not so much reach I guess because I only ever can just see him… and perhaps get a few words to him when he's in trouble."

"But I thought you said that you have helped him over roads and things Annie?"

"Yes sometimes that's right Cat, but I can only call to him, or maybe it's sort of will him to do things; I can't get down to him and lift him over things. Luckily at night when I find him the roads are always quiet and he seems to prefer creeping through the ends of peoples' gardens to going along roads."

"So how do you look after him in the day Annie when you are awake?"

"Well that's just it Cat, I can't of course, there's nothing I can do except pray for him.

"More and more as the days go by he seems to be getting into the routine of finding a house that will take him in early in the morning and feed him something, then let him sleep on a chair for the day. Come the evening he probably starts to get itchy feet; whatever happens he'll be chucked out before they go to bed Cat."

"It seems a funny time to be chucking him out... I mean at bedtime and stuff!"

"Well nobody wants to come down stairs in the morning and be greeted by a dirty great load of poo on their carpet do they?"

"Oh yuk, not half Annie... oh look Annie, there's your mum being chatted up by Lucy Worthing's dad at the swings!"

The girls giggle sexily, and both quickly think of things to say that will suggest they know all the ins and outs of chatting up.

They have reached the corner of the road that ascends into

the new housing estate. All the houses are little boxy semis, there's not one single big detached house amongst the lot of them, and many bigger buildings are split into one bed places for old folks or young couples starting out in life; or for one partner from young couples just having a divorce and needing to leave the family home.

Yes all of this is common currency on this estate; all the many shades of life can be found here.

"Hello Catherine…"

"Hi Mrs Sparks."

Lucy's dad grins hello at the two of them as they climb the hill to the swings, but clearly feels outnumbered now and chuckles something about wandering on up to see if his daughter's in sight yet.

As he walks away Annie notices how her mum is watching him go with soft but, sort of shining eyes.

"D'you like Mr Worthing Mum?"

"Hey… oh I see Annie; yes he's quite nice I suppose love… our gardens back onto each other, and as he works nights and wakes up mid morning, he often comes out into the garden with his first cup of coffee while I am putting the washing out or having a coffee in the garden myself when I come home from the shops."

Dee smiles at her curious daughter; she looks into dark eyes that hold her with innocent inexperience as might any young girl of her age; yet Dee feels her own inner thoughts are being looked at.

It is a little unnerving to find your private world exposed to the innocent but incisive scrutiny of your very own fairly young daughter.

Not that there is anything to worry about, the few over the garden wall exchanges have been friendly neighbour stuff… certainly no sultry pouting, or either allowing their eyes to go all big and moony.

All right… so just once when Dee was going to take her washing down to hang out, and have a friendly chat when he was out there; and because it was warm while she was working in her kitchen she had undone as she often does a couple of extra buttons on her blouse to keep cool; okay, admittedly as she was about to do them up before going down the garden, that time she decided to leave them undone for… well sort of for him really!

She did not think of it as sending any sort of specific sexy sign over the garden fence; if it was at all sexy, then it was because she was painting a picture of herself to the world that is Dee the desirable woman.

She likes to imagine herself as a beautiful heroine in a Spanish light opera… or in a passion filled low-budget film with guitars and castanets and flamenco dancing; or even a sort of weave of both, where she would have five beautiful children and herself be raven-haired and womanly… She would wear a long low fronted flamenco dress and have a wonderful contralto singing voice that can soothe all her children to sleep at night; bringing tall handsome men to her path outside to wait dark eyed and patient; leaning shadowed beneath moon-lit walls.

Yes... even just a bit of all that would be quite cool she thinks. For now, it will have to be enough just to imagine herself as some romantic suburban heroine; perhaps one day Annie will be just one of five beautiful children who she sings to sleep each night... but it will take a lot of singing lessons, because at the moment if she sings in the garden it makes all the dogs in the street howl!

Chapter Thirteen

Eggs

It isn't early... there again nor is it late.

He pads along with that anxious ears-back look that you will typically see when he is on the move in the daytime; at night he feels dark and invisible... so fairly safe.

He left that nice old lady's house on the council estate a couple of days ago. He had seen the orange fire of the evening sky over distant woods, and thrown like joyous paint plastered onto some crazy artists' canvas and it called to him. He felt a reassuring feeling that this distant golden world would bring him at last to his proper home and his proper life.

Their new house on the estate is forgotten already; he sees this evening glow leading to the archway and his courtyard... the courtyard where so many years before young Jake Jones lived in the loft above a stable... Sees his garden where he loves to creep round the bushes and then jump out on and run after his adopted brother who didn't know... well certainly who pretends he didn't know he was there.

He wants to be again where he can find Baskerville reversing down a tree and he'll come bounding up behind to take swipes at his tail.

Bobcat has moved on mostly at night, but sometimes also in the day if he feels awake and not too well fed. When he has eaten too many voles he tends to look for a nice dry bed of crisp dead leaves below a convenient bush to sleep it off.

Yesterday as it was getting dark he was stalking along the edge of a field towards the final dying glow of light in the sky, and above him a million pinhead points of glitter grew across the dark ceiling of his nocturnal world.

Stepping over a searching prickly arm of briar his landing pads register warmth. Looking down he sees nothing at first but the colour and pattern of leaves, yet there is warmth... then an explosion of wings and a blurted out 'chuck chuck chuck' of scolding voice, as a frantic partridge cannons' off into the night.

Bobcat having reared up with surprise himself, now lands again and something shoots out right from his clumsy paw with a cracking sound.

Bobcat still tracking the departure of his airborne Sunday roast doesn't bother to look at what he landed on.

The fading distant 'chuck chuck chuck' lands somewhere in the fragrant dark of the open field. Bobcat's paw lifts again to step forward, but at the same time a pungent eggy waft rises to his nose. At home if Dee is cooking omelettes for her family, as she cracks that first egg Baskerville always lets out a blood-curdling guttural yowl of realisation... he is just crazy about eggs.

At home Bobcat only really meows for eggs because hearing Baskerville's noise and always trusting Baskin's judgement, he assumes that these must be the most brilliant thing in the world that there is to eat. In truth, having joined his adopted brother for a few moments lapping at the yolk he usually wanders off and lets Baskerville finish it.

Though out here... out here where supper is never guaranteed, and every munchy vole it feels might be your last, the smell of a smashed egg means food, and is also the smell of home and Baskerville and Mum and Dad and Annie… and the safe routine of predictable treats.

Bob gets his head down to this sudden tasty blessing. He enjoys the flavour of his old safe life, and the slightly formed embryo in the middle makes a tasty addition; likewise he enjoys the novelty of lapping at an egg that is both raw and warm.

Snack finished he fails to connect with any thoughts of trying to crack another one; perhaps this encounter would have a different ending if the resourceful egg worshipping Baskerville were here tonight.

Bobcat licks his chops and ambles off.

He feels at peace with life, and these summer nights are always mild and mainly dry, and winter's chill is too far off to worry him yet.

The yellow sickle of the new moon that lit his way through railway wood two weeks ago has grown to a full glowing sphere of shining marble in the sky. As he tracks along the edge of the field it hangs there, but is moving increasingly from right to left ahead of him. He cannot reason that it means the edge of the field is turning gradually right, but something fundamental triggers his decision to go left into the forest.

Two beady eyes that have come quietly back through the hayfield see him slip between moonlit brambles and beyond concern.

The rather pessimistic partridge arrives at nest with jerking head and nervous stifled cluck that changes to a motherly crooning at the sight of five undamaged eggs. She circles round and settles down on them.

'The rather pessimistic partridge'

Two lie outside her downy breast,

So both are drawn in by hook of careful beak.

Nor does she spot that one in fact is cracked, so that will be that for its time on Earth.

Like this she settles for the night,

Though cannot know he'll not come back this way… at least not in this life.

As anxious eyelids droop, just one ear wonders where he's gone?

Where Bob slipped darkly into the wood, a faint mist tickles the brambled hedge along.'

Bobcat couldn't give a 'thingamajig' whether the partridge dozes serenely or anxiously, he's got some dirty great wood to worry about and that will keep him pretty busy for at least the rest of the night, and probably if things cut up rough, might take him the next couple of days.

His problem as well as danger, is all the complications and

distractions; woods would be easy if all you needed to do was creep into one end and navigate your way over, through, and under all that you encounter till you reach the other end. If however you find water you must try to drink enough in case it's miles till you find more. If you find a really peachy place to sleep it pays to have forty winks because it might be days before you find this quality of bed again.

If a litter of tiny plump baby rabbits cavort like mobile dinners in a dewy dingle, hopping delightfully about as they poo steaming bunny bullets beneath where silver birch droops

graceful arms to bless these little creatures of the Lord. If this happens, don't stop to pray, choose and pounce on one like there might be no tomorrow; if then to offer thanks you must, just do it as you lick your chops, and as God smiles down burp gratefully.

Two days on you scamper up some grassy bank through primrose on the lowest slope, then higher up you feel stalked by the stalks of lanky daffodils climbing the brow and nodding like a herd of tall golden giraffe in the cresting breeze.

An ivy festooned dying hazel tree holds its pose of disconsolation above him as he creeps with twitching nose up this bank of sweet scent. Bobby climbs the slope to find that beyond there is another steepish slope going back down again.

At the bottom of this grassy fall a tangle of azalea bushes make a colourful almost jungle canopy and reach to fences that mark the rear garden boundaries of a number of spacious and desirable bungalows. Bobcat desires only to see what can be in it for him.

When there are houses there are all sorts of possibilities, like suddenly finding you are home at last as trees and doors and pathways form familiar shapes. Even if you do not suddenly find you're home you might still find an open door, or the invitation to some food and a bed for the day.

A glance either way along the slope to check his path away from trees is clear of dogs and safe for now, he lopes with growing eagerness through tussocked grass and quickly down into the jungley darkness among the shrubs.

As you push around a now flowerless primrose, and duck beneath the final azalea limbs that sweep the wormy leaf-mould floor, your cat brain does not expect to be looking into the most gigantic bath that your world has known.

When he gets up at home on the dirty linen basket to watch Annie splash around in her bath with an old Barbie doll that for years she has been unsuccessfully teaching to swim, the bath looks enormous and deep but not frightening enough to stop him stretching his nose in to drink the lovely warm water.

But this is all quite different in this bath where you don't sit up on the edge and look down into the water; even before you get right up to it you are looking across an expanse of bath water where the morning breeze is pushing ripples along it, and is so full that it is brimming over onto the path as you approach. And why is there no one in it getting clean?

Nearer now his first thought is to drink some sweet warm water, even though there is no Annie in it to tickle him under the chin at the same time.

With paws already wet on the lapping edge he recoils from a brain-tingling fume that attacks his nose; he is not used to such a high percentage of chlorine, nor is this bathwater warm and smooth to swallow. He laps briefly for he has not found a puddle since the night before so he's very thirsty, but the strength of its fume makes him wonder what he's drinking and he 'knocks it on the head' but at least still alive.

The chlorine wouldn't have killed him, though it may have

made him woozy for a minute or so.

Now foot-by-foot enormous bath is left behind, and bungalow looms like an Aladdin's cave of opportunity below a small shrubbery.

But here a catch... no doors or windows open onto the garden, there again, no baying hound howls from inside, or even worse cannons murderous round the corner.

Bobcat stops and looks up at each window as if he thinks someone is going to hurl it open and any moment to call him inside. Nothing moves and he stands there with one paw raised and his eyes scanning any sort of window that look out onto the garden.

As a cat you don't stand waiting long because you can't work things out in any logical way; all you can do is note any opening or obvious possibilities, but if there is nothing you will just move on.

A driveway round the side of the house brings you to rose-beds and another lawn. He stops and sniffs the air... can almost taste the hint of food that wafts from somewhere... yes and also a sort of 'bedy' smell.

Bobcat peers longingly at the front windows of the house, but all as round the back are shut.

And then again comes that homely waft though clearly not from the house. The breeze has ruffled the fur on his right shoulder, he glances round and there he sees... an open door. It's nowhere you expect to find an open door, not out in a garden; not out here between rose-borders.

Four furry feet go pad pad pad, then to the step and sniff to check for dogs inside, but all seems clear so up and through he goes.

This house inside turns out to be just one room, but it seems to have everything even without going off through other doors.

Living rough for a week or so has made him develop a few bad habits that would see him given a clip round the ear if he practiced them at home. One leap gets him onto the work-surface by the sink; it is devoid of anything edible, in fact everything is in boxes on the floor.

The sink yields no nice defrosting chicken like he found in one big house a week ago; the woman wore very thick glasses and never did spot that one leg had been eaten half away; the guest who came for Sunday roast just assumed he had been required to share half his leg with someone else… which of course he had!

So no chicken, but the sink plug is in and the tap has earlier been run for a few seconds, so Bob gets the clean fresh water he needed.

Okay there's no food; not a big problem really because the summer woods are ringing with the squeaks of mice and voles so he's pretty well fed; the scavenger he has had to become however just cannot, not seek food at every chance.

When you have exhausted all the possibilities of finding food your thought switches to the next priority, sleep.

There are always beds of one type or another for a cat; what you have to do is simply select the best one. Bobcat peers up top to left, and then to right, and sniffing acutely as he does so as if he can judge their quality of comfort by their smell.

The eyes behind the sniff look undeniably demonic in their primeval search. The process somehow seems to click and he goes up to left; not lying straight down though, he goes round and round, and even stops to sniff again then round and round and flop.

This is his bed now. Whether he has ever been here before or has any sort of link to anything here is irrelevant. This bed is claimed as surely as when that same morning, the vole who's objecting head he bit off and swallowed was called his breakfast.

Bobcat shuts his eyes and breathes out one long sigh; the fresh air makes you sleep well!

Minutes pass and jaw quivers sporadically where whiskers twitch.

'In his dreams are images of woods and dogs...

of fields that must be crossed;

where the shouts of baying hounds echo through distant trees,

till cover broke the echo stops and you know you're on the menu...

and he is running hard again and again to be under the fence and safe up the trunk.

But now the image softens and he can see... Annie;

she is walking with his mum... that's her mum too.

The image fades and she is lost from view.

His slumber deepens and continues; at one moment there is a slightly rousing click that might have been a door,

just one ear twists reaching out from his dream...

...then nothing more.'

Chapter Fourteen

Caravan

Veronica and Ken are pleased to be on the road at last.

It always seems to take an age to get things done are packed and secure in their touring van.

When that's all done you suddenly remember any messages that must be left for the milkman and so on... yes like to call the paper shop so they don't send the papergirl up the hill with your magazines and stuff.

Ken is teasing Veronica about the amount of food she has brought with them, boxed up back in the caravan:

"Christ Ronnie, this old car feels very laboured coming up over the downs here, how many tins of beans have you brought with you?"

"Well we will be away for a little while Ken, and you know how grumpy you get when at odd times you are hungry."

"Yes but apart from breakfast we'll be eating out all the time. But never mind, we're almost to the top now then it's downhill into Dover... and it's pretty flat all the way to Paris."

First sight of sea looks pallid stretched and flattened, that at a glance you might think it was a huge car park. Even the outgoing and approaching ferries and the distant tiny white triangles of yachts becalmed along with their crew's fantasies of hanging heroically over the side against the gale are all seemingly so still… so still they lie you think that they have been forgot by time or consigned to be a picture… left sitting posed for a studio photographer who has retired.

"Isn't it funny Ken… as you come over the hill and look out to all those boats they seem to be just sitting there don't they?"

(There you are, I said that's how they look). But Ken is more worried about which tunnel train they will be in time for, and he squints at his watch with the look of someone who has good reason to want to be on a particular one.

In truth it really makes very little difference which one they catch because they know a nice campsite on the way to Paris, and it will be just as nice not to go the whole way today.

Twenty minutes later they are picking a path carefully through all the car-lanes and check points that will bring them to the holding point where they entrain.

There is a café and toilets, and as most of the people are holiday makers there is the happy sound of children trying to escape or evade their parents, who growl across the expanse of tarmac with gruff calls along the general theme of "Oy you lot, come back 'ere naa" etc, flung across the white lined playground, which is what the kids would see it as.

Ken and Veronica have no kids; they sit because of this a little quiet and pensive, and feeling something halfway between pleasure at these happy sounds, though envy too because they would perhaps have had their own had things been otherwise.

The wish for kids is mostly from Veronica... Ken has come to like his weekends free, so more feels relief that they can travel in freedom with nothing to complicate their trip.

Ken is screwing up his forehead to help him remember something.

"You look like you're thinking Ken... and because it's something you hardly ever do it really looks painful for you!"

"Yes very funny... for what it's worth, I'm trying to remember if I loaded my wellies. If this sky stays clear and we do have a night in a rural campsite on the way to Paris there will be a heavy dew when we get up tomorrow morning won't there."

"Ah so that's what you're taxing you tiny brain about love. Tell you what Ken, I want to have a look in that shop over there, I'll pop into the caravan and check things out for you as I go shall I?"

Ken nods in gratitude, with muttered thanks as Ronnie swings her legs out the door, in fact quite glad for an excuse to stretch them.

His hitherto lazy eye wakes up and takes a growing interest in life, as a slim young woman in a... well, just about what you could call a skirt goes past; and his rear springs dip and swell as Ronnie who seems to be taking her time in the caravan moves about in it.

He feels a final lurch of springs and click of door behind. Veronica comes back and crouches by his window with a slightly impish smirk across her face.

Ken smiles out at her:

"All right, don't tell me I've brought the left foot of two pairs and none of the rights?"

"No love, your boots are fine… everything seems to be in its place; even the cat seems quite happy!"

"Alright, so what does that word represent in the context of something we don't posses Ronnie?"

"What, cat? Oh it just means a small furry four-legged mammal with a long tail… though this one hasn't got a long tail, just a little stumpy one."

"Well, although you are clearly speaking some sort of gibberish Ron, it sounds as if there is something that you've done perhaps, or that you want me to go and sort out?"

"Yes I suppose you should really Ken."

Ronnie opens the car door as though she is a page-boy outside a posh hotel, and gestures with an extravagant sweeping motion of her arm towards the caravan.

She jumps up with both hands on the car, and twizzles round in mid air to sit on the bonnet, she swings her legs and feels again like a schoolgirl sitting on a wall to gossip with friends.

Ken is hardly in the caravan for fifteen seconds; the car lurches and the caravan door bangs shut as he hurries back…

"Christ Ronnie, there's a cat in our caravan!"

"Ah quick someone, award this man a degree in the bleedin obvious… go on, tell me something I don't know Ken!"

"Yes but how could it possibly have come to be in there?"

"Well… through the door I expect love."

"Okay clever, but what can we do with it now; I mean do we have to turn round and take it home or something?"

"But we don't even know where its home is Ken, I know it's not from anywhere near us. No, I reckon that now it's here it's got to take its chances with us for a couple of days, we can sort it out when we get home.

"I'll see what they've got in the shop here, but as there won't be much we can stop in Calais and get a litter tray and stuff."

"You sneaky devious woman, I think you're actually quite pleased we've got ourselves lumbered with this cat."

"Oh he won't be any trouble Ken… he'll just be locked in the caravan when we go off into town each night… hey look Ken, they've started loading, I think it's coming up for time to entrain."

"Are you sure it's a he… not that it makes a lot of difference really; what should we call him do you reckon love?"

"Well… he's black… and he must have jumped into our caravan like a jack-in-the-box, so it sounds to me like 'Blackjack' is as near as we will get to a name."

'Within an hour they're rumbling through the dark, though they don't see it's dark;

Inside the truck the light is hard and white, and just a jogging movement says they're going through the dark outside.

Twenty minutes more sees them explode… though just back into the sun again.

And France you feel has warmer soil, with village windows shuttered at the noon of day;

these villages where not a soul seems ever to be in the street…

What is so good to make them stay indoors, where and when do they meet?'

But on they charge and do not stop till Paris… 'ah Paris, Paris… where twice green the trees do salute the year' …and to a car park just beside the river Seine, because Ronnie wants to be at the top as it gets dark, of that great big fantastic tall thing that goes pointy at the crown, that often reaches to the clouds.

As lighted boats move slowly on the Seine with smoky diesel chug and cooking waft of floating restaurant… Bobcat lifts his nose his eyes till closed. The air through window has that weedy tang of riverbed combined with oily fume… a taste of sluggish peace.

> 'He sniffs the air, his dreaming starts,
>
> he's creeping through a dusty Sussex lane in quiet September,
>
> slowly night departs... and he is seeing Annie and his mum and dad again,
>
> and all the things that might have been had things been otherwise...
>
> Otherwise, what's otherwise? Had the Earth been a cube, or the Moon made of cheese?
>
> No not for a cat, he just wants things as they were.'

Had he only not felt that he should seek his proper home that fateful night, or perhaps he might have gone outside for a sniff around but shepherded by Baskerville, who always knows what not to do.

Now we see a little cat wake up, stirred by river smells and traffic sound and in the centre of a vast European city.

Bobcat hops down off the cushioned seat in the caravan, has a good drink of his water; that done he steps into the litter tray that Veronica bought him in Calais and doesn't half make the caravan whiff, but there you go!

Our romantic couple have wandered a little way along the bank of the river, and stopped in each other's arms to kiss and cuddle, perhaps a little inspired by the simmering lights of Paris; now they hold each other as darkness creeps through the 'twice green' trees, and both gaze up at the soaring heavenward rocket sweep of the Eiffel Tower.

"It's so beautiful Ken... each time we come here I still cannot believe it's real, and that it was built so long ago... and by all those tiny swarming climbing men."

"Yeah I know love… So, what do you think all those tiny swarming men were then Ron, Pygmies or dwarfs or something?"

"I mean they would have looked tiny from down here you plonker!"

Veronica stops grinning at Ken and jabbing his ribs etc, and looks back up at the fantastic tower; her eyes light with a different shine and her left hand lifts to her chin as demons tug at her shoulder making devilish thoughts ascend.

"You wander slowly on Ken, I'll just sort a few bits and catch you up."

Ken knows they often arrange to have short spells apart while they are away together, so doesn't say 'it's okay Ronnie I'll wait for you etc'; he ambles off across the park and the sinking sun makes shadows slide from shrub and seat.

Approaching the extraordinary iron ascent Ken feels so small and insignificant beneath its glory, but suddenly feels like a visiting celebrity when the lights all come on and it explodes into being a golden space-rocket just for him.

Ken stops by one of its four huge stolid yet finely poised feet in the growing twilight of the park; leaning like a mysterious stranger, sampling and approving the sweetness of the evening air.

He, who if we could get out of him what he thinks he looks like, would probably see himself leaning languidly with a typical French cigarette like 'Camel' or 'Gittanes' perhaps, except in fact he hates the very thought of breathing smoke.

Then as Ken floats in this fantasy, a perfect young Frenchwoman walks across the park and aims her path his way, and almost you might think as if she recognises so were coming to him:

'Each foot falls heel first with toes at 'ten to two',

Soft in its flat soled stylish Moroccan leather shoe… lands prettily in front of the preceding toe.

And softly so,

As soft, her skin is touched, or kissed, by twilight as she goes.'

With olive tone her skin is dark, bare shapely legs blue skirt and green voluminous nonchalant sweater; it all sounds a bit tat just spoke in words, but the resulting look is edible.

As the girl comes close and past, Ken finds two smiling eyes like glowing coals; one peeps mysteriously through a seductive confusion of dark tousled locks.

He follows in his dreams as she goes by, and 'saints above' she even turns her face and glances back.

This sort of brief encounter makes you flutter inside, and wishing you were here in France alone this time. He stares spellbound as she performs the perfect walk away… with exquisite articulation of her lower vertebrae…

'And Softly so...'

By MP.

"So there you are... why are you hiding from me in the shadows?"

The spell of course is thoroughly broke, and cracked his looking glass of hope, and through it his perfect French girl will walk away forever, though still held in his fragrant memory... a flower of possibility.

For a second Ken had forgotten Ronnie was on her way across to catch him up.

He straightens from his thoughts and observations of Parisian female succulence to eschew all pleasing speculation, and before Ronnie can ask anything too incisive he counter-attacks with,

"Hey, why the big holdall Ron, have you brought the stove and some tins of beans to eat at the top of the Eiffel tower?"

"Don't be silly all your life Ken… I've got our big coats."

"But it's so mild tonight Ron, it seems such a shame to be lumbered with stuff."

"Er yes, I know love, but we don't get up here very often and it will be such a shame to be driven back down if it's chilly when we are still watching the sunset, won't it?"

Ken agrees sort of, though still a little uncertain really as they go towards the kiosk for the lift and stairs.

"Shall we do the usual Ronnie, stairs to the first level then lift to the top? Oh mind you love, climbing with that bag will be no fun."

"Yeah that's true enough it will be a struggle, so let's go with the lift all the way today or we might miss the sunset; anyway I don't want to be too late getting to the campsite tonight love."

"Okay then… but hang on, so if we are having just a quick stop at the top what are the big coats for?"

"Oh I'll tell when were at the top Ken, if we keep talking about it we'll never get up there!"

Tickets paid for they ascend.

The stages one and two are passed.

The world sinks like the sinking ground around the airport when you fly off on holiday.

Being a quiet weekday evening there's no queuing as they go to the next lift at each level, in little more than minutes they are at the top.

You walk out a door into the high sweet air but it all feels wrong, because no one could be meant to be this high above the ground and yet un-winged.

The vista calls you to the wire… your breaths fall short and stall on your lips, it seems there is too much air about and you gulp fish-like.

It is only when Ronnie asks Ken if he will do the camera shots that she has planned that he starts to get a grip of himself.

"Yeah I can take some for you love."

They had taken loads the first time they came to the top, but on subsequent visits they have just marvelled at the view and committed it all to memory.

"Right there's the camera Ken… now when I say to start taking a few, just do it and ask questions afterwards okay!"

"Well sure Ronnie, but knowing you as I do this sounds like you've got something up your sleeve that I don't know about; hang on, you're not going to do some silly climbing up the safety fence or something I hope!"

But Ronnie has not gone to scrabble wildly up the fence 'or something', she crouches by the holdall and grips one end and begins carefully to drag the zip along.

"No please love, not a coat on, it will spoil the effect… your thin sweater looks well on you in this breeze!"

"Very funny Ken, but do something useful, point the camera and just get a shot of… this! Yeah, it's Blackjack, the world's first cat at the top of the Eiffel Tower."

Ken is open-mouthed but clicks away as ordered to; then from behind the camera comes in an incredulous tone,

"Jeez' Ronnie you're crazy bringing him up here, we can probably be locked up for the rest of our lives for this."

"Don't worry Ken, this is France; it's a people's republic where they chop the heads of kings and queens and aristocrats, but almost anything the peasants do is okay."

"Yes, but remember that you're a peasant whose country has spent a thousand years fighting them!"

Bobcat for his part just likes being out in the wind again, and at the same time cuddled by his latest mum.

His eyes aren't used to being miles away from things, so the enormous fall to the city lights has little effect and does not really register with him as being from a great height.

Then to the west he sees that sinking orange glow, and thought clicks back to where his journey ends.

A bit like an otter who has seen a fish, his head points forward and focused for a moment then… he relaxes in new Mum's warm embrace, and the Indian couple just along the fence throw sparkling eyes and stunned surprise to find a cat outside up here.

They smile, and in impressive English she makes a joke about 'letting the cat out of the bag', then asks if it's okay for them to take a few shots too. And a man from round the other side who was photographing the city with a very big expensive looking camera takes a few as well.

Veronica carries Bob slowly to the fence as Ken takes pictures; she is still a little afraid he will suddenly realise how high he is and panic. At the fence his neck extends like an otter again. Bob is staring down from this branchless tree… are those tiny moving things on the forest floor mice or ants, and why are there no other trees with birds singing across to birds elsewhere.

Ronnie kisses the top of his confused little head and smiles lovingly at her adopted friend.

Bobcat's eyes lifting from this amazing forest floor are drawn again to the sinking red glow of the set sun… does he wonder if he's almost home now? Can his tarmac drive and trees and archway and courtyard be just beyond the dying coals of the now sunk sun.

Out east high across the city behind them, twinkled points of silver light grow seething in the darkened grey as night arrives.

Paris ce soir, glows and simmers like an extraordinarily

active dream far below their lofty perch.

They may never be up here again but moments stretch out to questions, and something says it's time to go back down.

Let out of bag,

the cat is now put back…

…and Ken and Ronnie go below.

Chapter Fifteen

Wrestling

"Oh yes of course, I've just worked it out now Dee."

"And what's that then clever clogs?"

"Why you were making up that story to get Annie into bed early tonight... you want to watch that sexy serial without her calling down the stairs, or coming down and peeping though the crack in the door when you've started getting a bit naughty."

"Don't be silly Mike, I took her up early because she's been out on a field trip all day. What's more, it's generally you who starts any fun and games.
"Anyway, I was still tidying a few bits around in her room and talking to her when she began snoring."

"Yeah well, your voice has that effect on me too love!"

From Dee and Michael's point of view life is fairly back to normal now. The loss of Bobcat is for the two of them an accepted permanent fact; though something that is still referred to as an ongoing search if they are talking to their daughter.

Baskerville lifts his sleepy head and winks big eyes at them from his extra spacious place in front of the glowing fire. He cannot see his adopted brother in his mind's eye; but when during the day Mum opens a tin of food Baskerville runs through expecting to bump noses with Bobcat at the bowl. As he eats without having to alternate noses in competition anymore, it just means his life is a little easier.

Basky is vaguely aware that there will be no more coal added to the fire tonight, though not because he knows they always take an early night straight after the sexy serial! He just knows that after certain sounds and smells float round the room they go to bed.

It's fine with him for as the fire dies and they go up, he just swaps to their lovely hot spot on the sofa.

Mike and Dee both think about their departed cat from time to time, though mostly when in the morning Annie tells them one of her frequent and recurring dreams. She often gives such clear accounts of where he was in terms of her description of these places that it sometimes really makes them wonder. Though putting a name to the locations is much harder.

Quite a few times now to please their little girl they have all three gone off on a search. Once she had described a railway station with a huge gas storage tank behind it; Annie said Bobcat had been dozing through some of the night on a sheltered grassy bank beyond the station footpath.

Mum and Dad never know quite what to think about their daughter and her stories; if it's a nice evening though it can be quite fun to go off in their van to look for somewhere she has described. But they went in search with her this time as much to show they listen to her and care; town railway stations it must be said are not the most inspiring places for a 'rece'.

Annie took them up and over the footbridge and beyond the footpath was indeed a grassy bank. Annie headed straight to one end of the bank and after a brief search said 'this is where Bobby slept'.

Dee and Michael came along to where their daughter knelt and in front of her was a nest of pressed out in the long grass. Of course both knew it might just as easily have been the bed of some stray dog or other cat… nor did they think to search the grass for a tuft of fur to have forensically tested and matched. But the way she took them to the spot was so confident.

Of course by the time they had got there, just before tea-time, it was the day after he was there… if he ever was.

Mum and Dad take Annie's quest seriously enough for them to have pinned an old map up on Annie's bedroom wall. As best they can they have been marking all their little girl's sightings on the map. These cannot be described as going in anything like a straight line; the only unifying factor is that each one is further west than the one before.

The sexy serial is getting under way although no one is being naughty yet or wrestling without pyjamas when they should be going to bed!

Mike and Dee snuggle lower on the sofa. Mike gives Dee a squeeze and suggests she might make life rather easier if she were to undo some of her clothing before the 'kick-off'. He receives a thumb-jab in the ribs, but then Dee wriggles closer and slides her hand up his tee-shirt.

The TV flickers in the dark of the room as several characters bicker about something and stomp around. At last you start to hear a few saxophones beginning to wheeze and there seems to be more prospect of some serious action getting under way. Mike's eyes lift to the ceiling, and hoping this change in the music won't bring their daughter back down on some pretext or other.

A tall dark muscular young male and a very succulent looking auburn haired female have arrived home still apparently fuming about whatever the argument had been about with the other two couples.

Of course as usual in the series, any active discourse or dispute seems to get everyone's hormones all buzzing and almost as soon as they get up stairs and begin to undress for bed, they start wrestling... or whatever.

Not wanting to waste a minute Mike turns and cuddles up to Dee with sneaky fingers:

"Hey not so fast lover-boy, I thought you said it was me liked all this stuff?"

Dee knows that what will be will be, nor would she want it any other way. Then as the music falls to a moody pulse the clear and troubled tones of Annie's sleepy weeping filters down-stairs and through the crack in the door.

"Oh my giddy aunt, not now Annie... quickly love, go and sort her out before she gets really upset."

"Hang on Mike, why am I the one to go and sort her, she's just as much your daughter."

"Yes but you've talked to her about Bobcat much more often than I have, like as you're coming home from school and stuff, so you're more likely to say the right thing to shut her up."

"Well maybe it's got nothing to do with her cat, what if she's crying because she wants her daddy? And what's more... 'Shut her up'! So is that how you see it Mike, is our little girl just an inconvenience that needs 'shutting up'!"

"No Dee, you know I... oh bugger it I'll go and see what's the matter."

Dee grins triumphant and settles back to her TV; but knowing also that Mike will expect some 'special' treatment when he's sorted things upstairs.

It feels rather nice now to be left down here alone; alone except for her little mate Baskin, and both relax in the flickered firelight.

Her sexy serial wrestles and nibbles its way to a supposed temporary climax, and leaving Dee with a tingle down her spine, and plans for when her man gets back downstairs.

Thoughts that, should she go up and stop him coming down again, are beaten by the warmth of her toes stretched out towards the glowing coals... though only just beaten. If Mike wants some sort of 'lerve' when he gets back down again it's only on if she can keep her feet facing the fire.

Soon a dump dump dump descends the stairs and Mike appears with a 'this was something a little bit different' raised eyebrowed look across his face, and a 'you won't believe this' tilt of his head.

"All quiet on the western front now love?"

"Yes fine Dee, but she was quiet as I got up to the top of the stairs. I nearly came straight down again, but being such a devoted father I peeped in to check she was all covered up and spoke a few words.

"Her eyes were open and she said quietly 'it's all right now Dad, when I found Bobcat he was being held by a woman I have never seen him with before, and they were at the top of a tall tower in the middle of some huge city. I've seen it lots of times in pictures but I can't remember where it is.

"I was going to ask if she thought she would remember where it was this high tower, but she carried on quickly…

'Then the lady started walking towards the edge of this high tower and I was scared she might be going to throw him over but I couldn't seem to warn him.

'It was alright, she only wanted him to see the view, and to let her husband take photos of her with Bobby.'

"Then after she had told me all that Annie went quiet, so I just kissed her and came back down stairs, but what do you make of all that Dee?"

"I know what I reckon Mike… I reckon we have one very imaginative daughter, and one day she will make us all very rich… somehow."

"Yep and I'll drink to that as well Dee, least I would if someone had remembered to get me some tins from the supermarket, but in the absence of a nice beer I will have to make do with the second best treat!"

Affectionately he strokes the back of Dee's neck, but with a subtle pressure; and Baskerville hears familiar sounds that mean he soon will get his favourite bed.

Chapter Sixteen

Going Home

Today the usual cheesy feet and grunty noises clump and bump around the caravan.

It looks as if as other days he'll be left here with litter tray and food and water sun-dozed on his comfy bench; though first let out on campsite grass while they give him breakfast, and allowed to scamper about a bit... yesterday he even made it up a tree nearby to lounge lion-like on a branch while the Jack Russell terrier in the caravan behind them went berserk and its dad hurled sundry shoes at it to try and shut it up.

This morning-freedom always ends with him shut in the van for the duration of his adopted mum's day out... though they never go for a whole day; these things have been the routine of his recent past.

His people never let him play outside 'as evening spreads her sail across the sky'. What do they know? Bob often stares out through the caravan window at this somnolent sinking glow, it sometimes says he should be moving on. He's got no great sense of distance or direction, but knows his home is somewhere near the orange bit.

Now the sun has gone all the way round and come back up again.

'This morning comes with much upheaval, pots are stacked and cups are stowed,

some things that vaguely may or may not even have a function... find a home.

Bob is put out for his morning scamper, he seems to always get a run before they drive.

And because it's always them who drive away he expects today a lazy time confined to barracks.

French days are warm, but van is under trees with windows wide...

...ah yes but no way out because mosquito nets mean he's confined.

Then what is there a cat can do, but sleep and eat and drink... and poo!'

It is with some surprise that after being put back in from his scamper about, he does not hear them drive away as he subsides toward sleep, and instead there comes the bump and clunk of the tow hitch locking down, combined with eager winding under van of corner jacks.

"Do you want me to wind the last one up Ken, you look completely shagged!"

"Yeah okay love that's not such a bad idea. I'm sure we could easily get away with only putting one down at each corner really, but you can be sure that some ponsy caravan club nerd would come and try to tell us we're doing it wrong, and how much strain or harm etc."

"I know Ken... it's the only drawback to camping with a van isn't it... I mean the sort of people who do it. Hey you don't suppose we're that type do you?"

"Heavens no, we're nothing like them at all, we've got all our own ways of doing things love."

"What things do you mean?"

"Well... well we've got Blackjack with us when most people have children and dogs; er... then I suppose like how many corner jacks we wind down."

"Yes, but we always wind all four down."

"Well so far yes we have... but we may not always, so in some senses we don't always... sort of in the future tense and sense Ronnie!"

> 'So up the final jack is wound and they have gone.
>
> Green whispering lanes soft-verged by whispering rye grass make wishing washing ripply walls that seem to... whisper?
>
> And sunlight flickers through a thousand trembling aspen fingers of the poplar tree.
>
> France feels to be tempting their swift return... or is it somehow, not to leave.'

Veronica lounges as they drive slightly dry mouthed after two good bottles (shared) of merlot while they sat out before bed in the silken night.

Now the sun has just snuck past its zenith for they don't

want to set off home too early from their sojourn in France. They mostly like to pace the drive back so they can catch a ferry and be up on deck in the sunset; if need be a few diversions can be found along the way to hold them up a bit.

She lounges there settled but slightly broody in the front seat as they drive, initially it feels not for children; sure if one showed up she'd happily make the best of it. She sits and thinks her thoughts of keeping Blackjack, that's why she feels broody.

However all that said, a caravan of kids she imagines would also be a happy van; she sees them down in Cornwall playing on the Padstow sands where shallow golden water sparkles warmed by sun.

'France feels to be tempting their swift return'

Seagulls call above dune grass that makes low whistle in the gentle wind, as their children splash in sandy pool.

The twins, one boy one girl, for that she always thought is what they'd be, now rumbly tummied vote for hot-dogs.

She smiles and sees them trooping back to town, the four of them across the sand... all hand in hand.

Her eyes and thought drift back to now:

'Another dusty crumbly shuttered village looms,

Its stony cobbled street echoes their careful passage through,

Then out beyond and back into the summer fields.

Wheat sways stroked firmly, lusciously, where a warm wind swells beyond the grassy banks;

While small bright flowers cluster ardently to nod and smile in sun,

As if counting their brief season... almost done.'

Quiet jolting lanes find faster highways running straight.

With all windows shut and now just the vents, Bob finds the air inside is warm; he stretches relaxed and gently rocked by motion of the motorway.

The climbing morning sun now through the window finds his black fur and gets to work on it. He rolls and stretches feeling this is something to celebrate, but after a bit more of this he will no doubt be sent below the bench onto the floor to cool off.

Phew yes, this preponderance of sunlight starts to feel like he has gone a bridge too far in his search for perfection, now it's only habit that keeps him in the hot bit; you can see his paws reaching out to feel their way towards a cooler post.

Were a wafting breeze to stroke his fur this sun would feel like luxury, but here... here it's really just a bit too much to bear.

And now it comes, that lolling sloping slide with eyes still closed, of head and shoulders over edge as a sea-lion slides off rocks when the keeper appears with his bucket of fish at feeding time.

Beneath the bench-seat on the carpeted cool floor he stretches out with the smell of plywood and rubber gas pipe. Bobcat's chin jiggles gently as its weight is supported on the minutely oscillated pile of the carpet.

Now here they slow through a town and come to red traffic lights; there is a woman with two dogs on the pavement hardly more than a few yards away… or as we are in France 'metres'; if Bobcat stuck his nose above the parapet would he jump back with shock?

The next lights are on the outskirts of Calais. As they sit waiting there Veronica glances out and slightly back to the left. A youngish male with dark curly hair and crafted leather cowboy boots reclines on a green bench with the languid air of a man who has confidence in his place in this world, and control of his destiny.

Ronnie looks at his confident poise and handsome thoughtful eyes, and she wonders if their fleeting paths will ever cross again in this life.

He might almost have picked up her thought or at least her eye, for now he smiles in at her with a warmth and intelligence that makes her lips soften and part slightly in a careful smile of her own.

No single muscle or tendon has moved or adjusted its tone more than a few microns, yet thought flows back and forth between two people's worlds of separate safety.

Gallic male smiles sweetly at Ronnie, yet discretely… he tilts his face to one side and lifts his rather heroic chin as his lips form maybe to speak, then part and gently mouth and pass a kiss to her.

Ronnie's eyes dilate so well you could almost fall into them; she feels held by something powerful and primeval, and all the nerves in her body bristle... some even more than others... and smiling back like a grateful child that has just received a gift at Christmas... then the lights go green, as she goes hmm... and life alas reluctantly slides safely on.

Thought for Ronnie does not switch as easily to other things as do go lights from red to green; she is as many women are just driven away, but holding the art of her thought like her best picture achieved at last winter's watercolour painting class.

Ronnie knows that she had just been blessed by perfect moment, over which any reality she might have had with him would have thrown a shade of dullness.

The surge and lagging clonk of the pulled caravan brings her thought to where she really is and who she really is; though who she also really is, is still smiling, and knowing it was the most fun encounter of her life; and her best moment too I suppose you could say.

A few more sets of lights and the shops have been and gone and fields return, and road to ferry port runs on.

"Think we'll have to wait long love, or will we drive straight on to the ferry?"

"Just give me a second to polish my crystal ball and I'll tell you Ken!"

"Alright clever clogs; look I can just drive and say nothing to you if you prefer us to sit in silence all the way…"

Veronica grins at him and tickles his knee, though she would in fact quite like to return in her mind to what she had just been doing with her Gallic male.

Now Ronnie's spell however is thoroughly broke, her looking glass of hope is cracked, and the web of possibility and intrigue hangs in tatters here; any subsequent returns will be increasingly more fraught… though maybe she will try to get back to her Gallic male after Ken has been snoring for a while tonight!

If tonight he does not want too soon to snore, and needs a cuddle, then as occasionally girlfriends have advocated, she will imagine he's her Gallic-Male.

An amiable silence pervades in the car while.

Bobcat comes back to Veronica's attention:

"Oh what about Blackjack Ken… do you think he needs to stretch his legs, you know have a run about before we join the queue for the boat?"

"No love, he's a cat not a race-horse; they spend on average well over half their lives asleep… and would probably spend even more if they could, so he'll be as happy as Larry back there."

"When we get him home, I wonder what he'll want to do?"

"I expect he'll toddle off back to his house."

"No I hardly think so… apart from our little cul-de-sac of bungalows there's hardly another house for miles."

"Yes but the house on our side just before the lane has got fairly new people in it, he could be theirs… or one maybe of our neighbours could have taken on a rescue cat in the last week or so, and he was just out exploring all the gardens when he found our open caravan."

"Yeah I s'pose he could be local… But if he's from miles away and no one has a clue about him do you think we should…"

"… I was just going to say Ron, that I could feel you working your way round to finding reasons to hang on to him!"

"Not really to hang onto him Ken, I just hate to think of him lost and alone out there… or taken to a cat rescue home and eventually old and forgotten in a wire cage at the end of some kind lady's garden.

"Can we possibly allow that to be the end of the story of Blackjack, the first cat to the top of the Eiffel Tower?"

"The first as far as we know!"

"Well okay then, as far as we know."

"I know it's not just up to me Ron, but I am scared to commit myself to the idea of keeping him; I feel we've got to keep an open mind about his future or we may talk ourselves into something that is really not such a great idea... Hey look that's lucky, just as we're driving in they've started to let them on!"

They have arrived at Calais ferry port and Ken shows their ticket and gets waved straight through to join the queue of caravans.

He turns to his woman:

"Tell me Ronnie, do you reckon there will ever be a day when you will think it's safe to go both ways in the tunnel, or both ways on the boat? A return ticket could save us a lot of money!"

"If you weren't so tight we could save that money now, because if we went more often we could buy two return tickets, and use half of one to go there, and half of the other to get back... then next time vice versa."

"Or even easier Ron, why not go there and back on the boat one week, and the train a month later."

"That's no good... what happens if there's a bomb in the tunnel, we'd be doubling our chances of being in there when it goes off. Or if the boat doesn't sink on the way over it might on the way back!"

Ken knows he's on a hiding to nothing with this one... knows that his logic and Veronica's logic are not just opposite sides of the same coin; the two sides are as foreign as two different sides of two foreign coins.

All the first rows of cars have gone on and it's the turn of all the towed caravans. They rumble down the ramp because it's low tide and the boat is sitting low on the dock, and to a crewman who gestures them along a lane to park.

Both out in the hollow ringing dinginess of the car deck, they stand aside from the exit gangway to let people pass them to get to the stairs.

"Have you got anything you want to take upstairs Hun'?"

"Yeah, but tell you what love… I'll see you up there; I want to sort a few bits in the van and talk to Blackjack for a minute before I come up on deck… is that okay?"

"It's good actually Ronnie, it will give me a chance to size up the talent on my own for a change!"

"Okay, but don't expect any miracles love… I should concentrate on the ones wearing very thick glasses if I was you."

"Right you, come here and kiss me, or lose me!"

Ken is kissed and naughtily fumbled, then lopes off to climb upstairs to the passenger deck.
A few other people are still on their way up, but most have made it to the cafeteria, or to have a fag out on deck.
The time to sail towards blighty is almost come.

Grumbled massive prop shafts turn shedding tortured grease, as all flat metal sheet vibrates and submarine cavitatious millwheels chop and churn.

A floating block of flats moves off the dock and jetties roar and slap with thundered side thrust blast that swirls and plunders pissed-off whelks and mussels; and slimed green timber baulks shout back a raucous rendition of this chaotic song.

Ken breasts the upper deck and makes the outer promenade… and gulps deep gusts of channel wind. Later after they pick up a Turkish take-away in Tenterden, he will get home and in reply knock out a generous blast or two of wind himself.

'Bobcat put in dark once more, feels jolt and jiggle, noise and nudging, sometimes light and sometimes heavy.

Sometimes scent to nose arrives, and often voices rise… and fall till Ken's gruff welcome and a kissing sound.

Buzz and rip of zip across, and flood of light and gulp of channel wind,

and his new mum's warm clutching arms around.'

"Yeah here we are Ken, it's Blackjack, the first cat on the top deck of a cross channel ferry!"

(and it is more likely to be true than it was up the Eiffel Tower)

There's the sinking sun against the flecked Cirrus of an approaching wet English weather front, so he must be getting nearer his journey's end now mustn't he?

Chapter Seventeen

Jake in 1917

Annie's dream life still sometimes finds the echo of Jake and Disraeli; not always in tones clear or coherent to her, though to Jake his situation back then at the outbreak of the Great War became as clear and unavoidable as anything he had ever imagined he would have to face.

Jake sits in a chair not himself grey or shivered but smiled on by the kind old sun, and blessed by scent of peaty breeze that wafts cosily down off the early summer moor.

He's got big wheels so if need be he can wheel away, or some kind soul can come and push him quickly under cover when the moorland rain begins to fall. In his rather sickly state a nasty chill might start a cough that puts him in bed, then pneumonia if he's there too long is just a splutter away!

He can get along by himself with his crutches but he hasn't made as much effort to get familiar with them as he might have done, because there is the promise soon of his very own wooden leg.

Jake visualises himself walking soon again to the Masons Arms in Camelford, with his hands shoved confidently into his pockets and not even a stick. Just lately though he's not been coming on as well as he had hoped; he knows he's been sitting around too much but just hasn't really felt like doing a lot.

It is hard to imagine anyone looking forward to a wooden leg, unless like him you haven't got a leg at all… he is eager to see it because he feels it will get him fired up to get on with his life; he wants to know what of all the old stuff he did he will still be able to do when he has it.

His kind employers at the big house have promised to let him return to whatever work it turns out he can do. He knows they were probably pushed that way somewhat both by a sense of patriotic duty, and their beautiful flaxen haired daughter Judith.

Judith is not just a flaxen-haired beauty who liked to bring out a cool lemonade to their handsome houseboy; she is practical and resourceful too.

She loves things mechanical, like the motorbike and sidecar that she pleaded with her parents to buy, that now has given her the freedom of moors and local town.

At sixteen she was all horses and jodhpurs, then she saw her first motorbike and it was love straight away.

Warmth slides down the moss-patched roofs… and even time slides too perhaps?

A cat recumbent, lounging by the village drinking trough for horses, rolls in sun; and upside down sees butchers shop with pigs hung upward The handsome young suitor from a wealthy family with an estate near Padstow, thinks she would be safer and more 'future wifely' secure at her parents home with embroidery work and pets to walk; but he is away with the navy most of the time.

So now with Judith's new found freedom on three wonderful wheels, and with the tingle that she gets in helping Jake be rehabilitated into parts of his old life; for these you often see her riding into the village of a morning to check on him.

Judith is a couple of years older than Jake, so lets that be her excuse to play the mother hen. She might even sometimes help him get across the street and to use the toilet, which he likes, although he can get across well enough alone; or Judith might insist she be allowed to check his stump is healing well and not going septic again; she always brings her armoury of creams and cleansing lotions from her parent's house.

Sometimes his stump has been sore and oozing pus for a few days and she must set about it like a devoted big sister, for it has to be completely healed to be any use with a wooden leg.

Jake enjoys this fuss and attention and has even rubbed and worried his wound around a bit when he knows she may arrive.

If Judith appears in the village early, and he hears that paff paff paff of her motor coming down the high street, then a swift judicious hand of spit can help the stump to look a bit sore and weepy to curry her sympathy.

Now sitting in his ghastly grey de-mobilisation suit he is glad at least he didn't lose his hands… as someone he was with in the field hospital in France had:

'Now he will never feel again how slim girl's waists are… or how warm their subtle hands!'

"Just think"

He muses…

"Never even being able to wipe your own bum again!… I'd rather have lost both legs, one arm, and my sight, than have to have my bum wiped… unless perhaps Judith… yes I suppose if it was always the same hand it would sooner or later just be like your own.

"Hey but what when she's not there? Then you might have to have some patriotic but rough handed old farmer do it for you… Christ I've really been so lucky."

It's pretty good if you can come home from a war and you still feel you have been lucky; yes Great Britain needed young lads who asked few questions.

Today the sun tilts warm and scarcely cloud scud in an azure sky; the from what appears the floor… but still smelling the right way up.

He also hears four wood rimmed wheels make laboured voyage on the dusty way.

Bringing his world 'sky up' again, cat sees Jake push at rim of wheels to roll across as learned from other days that this is movement worth latching onto.

Jake gets to the pollarded high street elms and halts by the horse-trough.

"Ah, so you're here again Ginger old mate, I suppose you hope you're in with a chance of a crunchy corner of my pasty?"

Jake smiles down on this big old ginger tom's up-staring face; he knows he charts Jake's daily movements to the butcher's shop… the shop that's known to bake the best pasties for miles.

If someone from one of the big houses comes, or a traveller stops for pasties they're a penny each, but for villagers or Jake they're a ha'penny… sometimes if one burns a bit, that's his for free.

Jake shifts about on his cushioned seat to find some relief for his pressure sores, then reaches down to Ginger and jibbers his first and middle finger under his chin. Ginger likes the touch and turns his head on side to maximise coverage; but counting also seconds till this human will go wheeling on to butcher's shop to call for pasty.

Jake looks down at this worldly-wise old tom suddenly remembering his own, and thinks about Disraeli. He left him to live out his years at the big house in Kent, and to catch mice and rats as he loved so much to do. There was no way he could have made the journey too; neither led on lead nor carried in box… no his life was better passed with the new stable boy in his same old courtyard.

Yet Jake still sees him sneaking through the straw of the stable below his attic trap door; and with the devilish cunning of at least five cats; and seeing rat creep out, but waiting till it gets away from any hole or cover till he springs.

Jake straightens up from Ginger to push on wheels, and rolls along to butcher's shop to call through door. Most amputees from the war just get simple chairs with wheels attached to them, in case they don't live long enough to warrant anything more sophisticated. They have to be pushed to a sunny spot by some kind person; but Judith took it on herself to pay to get one made for Jake with big wheels on each side that you can push with hands to get yourself around.

Then Jake outside the butcher's door shouts:

"Hey Jim, you got the next tray of pasties out the oven yet mate?"

And Jim who halts hatchet high and poised like a pedantic executioner seeking the perfect spot to re-slam cleaver through the splintering spine of a pig's neck calls out:

161

"I'll bring you one out Jake, don't run away… or roll away!"

"Yeah very funny Jim; yes and sniff it to see it's one with plenty of meat in it, not all potato and swede like yesterday can you!"

Pasty brought out by Jim smells good, and Ginger's led by nose to come and to rub against leather booted ankle.

Jake thanks well-fed butcher boy and parts with a ha'penny from his King's pension… he wonders why he sold his leg for so little? But finds also that the dreams of all that he will do with his new leg come surging on:

He will stride across the Padstow sands through sun and spray, break wind at will, and burp like man who clearly likes a beer with mates… yes, that again as well… to stand at bar of Masons Arms and belch with pride and confidence, see barmaid glancing heavenward, trying to look meek and shocked as though she never does the same.

'He thinks he'll make a good home as the work builds up… and better still, secure a tasty wife; then children who he'll love to love, and love to see them growing up from kiddies playing on the sand, to jobs and homes and later children of their own.

He cannot know…

he must not know…

at least it would be better he does not…

that seven years will see him down to half his weight, with poisoned stump, and thinning blood, his hopes and erstwhile dreams at last run down to 'a bitter cud of vile incurable sores'…

…and Judith's tears when he is gone.'

"And Judith's tears…"

Yes, Judith's tears when he is gone…

Chapter Eighteen

The Journalist

Numerous rumbling yorks of mail sacks straight off the dock come wheeling through pushed by an army of casuals, and wheeled towards another standing army of yet more casuals who cut and tip and cut and tip, and 'seg' and sort and sort and 'seg' throughout their shift.

Michael Sparks works mainly at the other end of this vast Post Office mail centre; he's with all the machines and conveyor belts and other gadgets. This end employs a multiplicity of minions.

Through the transparent flaps of doors that lead outside he sees lorries lining up to drop their load; or freshly loaded firing off into the creeping dark.

Behind him huge rotating drums are fed by conveyor belts of flicking falling letters; machines aspiring somehow to get these letters right way up and send them on to clever jabbered whirring wheels and belts and magic eyes that read the postal codes.

Half the guys who work here all their lives will never understand how these huge contraptions live and breathe; they climb the steps of the dock to come and do their time each day or night; then tramp away to spend some hours at home, or stopped off at pub, and later run the gauntlet of disgruntled wife.

Michael Sparks is engineer and knows his stuff. He sorts out jammed machines and can quickly tell if it's a motor burned or just a fuse; and guys with broke machines will call for him because he never points the finger of blame at the postal staff like grouchy Colin with his bulging sweaty form and sulky stance.

But now it's nearly break time leaving just two hours till the final bell and then he's free to run for home.

As the supervisors give the shout they troop off to the rest room Alan calls to Michael:

"Get your coffee mate and come down the end table, I got a question; and a picture that will interest you even if it has no connection with your stuff."

Michael grins and nods, and as he gets his coffee at the counter wonders what Alan refers to when he says 'stuff'.

At Alan's table, first they only speak of football, with who's most likely to go through etc.

As that is dealt with and sorted by the pair, Michael's thoughts return to his mate's comment about 'connections with 'Michael's stuff'.

"So anyway mate… you were saying before we got onto football that there was something you had seen I think, or something to show me?"

"Yeah of course Mike… hang on, where's the photo. But first off… you did say one of your cats is still missing didn't you?"

"Fraid so, but Annie hasn't given up on him yet; me and Dee are not sure what to think."

"And it is that black one with the sort of Siamese face I'm assuming… looked a bit like one of mine except with no tail, is that right?"

"Yes I suppose it is like one of yours a bit."

"I thought it was… anyway Mate, some English journalist was doing an article about Paris and was taking evening photos at the top of the Eiffel Tower. A woman also at the top had a big zip up holdall from which she produced a cat that she had apparently taken up to show the view.

"Fair enough Mike, she must have been absolutely barking mad, but there you go! So my old woman picked it out in the paper because the cat looked a bit like that black one of yours… Yeah this is it, and he took it from quite close up. But you can't see if it's got a tail or not because of how she's clutching it."

"You know Al that's really strange… okay, I know there's no possible way it can be Annie's Bobcat, and being taken up the Eiffel Tower by some mad French woman… but it is still really like him, and even stranger…"

"No mate, that's part of why I thought of you… the woman was English not French… well so the journalist reckons in his piece. Yes and after he had done some shots he must have asked her the cat's name for his notes and… look it says it down here, hang on… em, yes here… 'we call him Blackjack'; me and Jill both reckoned it almost sounded a bit like she'd only just given him that name."

"Well yes Al, but as I was about to say, that not only is there a startling similarity of the cat's face, well as much as you can see… but also that not long ago Annie saw him in a dream with a woman, and at the top of a big tower which she had seen pictures of though didn't know where it was."

"Now that is pretty spooky mate! Hmm… mind you Mike?"

Al hunches over the picture with his head on one side.

"What've you seen there?

"Well perhaps the woman was barking mad… but she looks all nice and chilly in the wind high up there and wearing that clingy top… if you know what I mean, doesn't she!"

"Funny, but I was just thinking more or less exactly that too Al!"

With that their thoughts slide away from Annie's cat, to park themselves and dally in an area more central to their male psyches.

That evening with his Friday late shift done Mike heads for home head full of heady thought.

In the staff car-park a swarm of headlights push to get their nose towards the security gate and exit, and things that link his daughter's dream to something that might really be, to mind are brought.

It all seems too fantastic yet it seems to fit in some strange way. And all these bits are pushed around, and hoping that his Annie's dream will find some link today.

She'll be in bed asleep of course, and Dee most probably snoring likewise. He will leave Al's newspaper down stairs and can get the two of them together over breakfast.

Mike thinks about his women folk demanding an outing to search the streets of Paris for Bobcat, and gulps a little as he brings to mind the meagre balance of money in their current account.

The car park barrier lifts; the security lads know and never check him so he's through and off and down the road where others stream shift finished for another week.

Mike checks his watch... his dreaming stops... and thoughts of beer, and scent and glow of a dreamed sweetness course his veins. Dee likes to see him slip the leash on Friday night, it means when he on other shifts is there at home for Annie, she can have a night out with her friends.

So all that said, with time to grab a pint or three he swerves away from High Street to the Brewers Arms!

Chapter Nineteen

The Morning After

If he ever sees him again he will remember that he knows the smell and shape, though no doubt be quite wary for a little while.

She brightens like a bee that's just found sweet marigolds with honeysuckle dangling above f

"Hello love… you slept in late today! Was it a hard shift to tire you out so much?"

"Yeah that's right Dee."

"And is the van playing up again, I thought you had it all sorted now… did you have to leave it at work?"

"Oh I see what you're driving at now… No I stopped off at the 'Brewers' for a swift half on my way home."

"Oh so you weren't that tired then… and you should have been safe driving home love, they wouldn't nick you for a half pint of beer!"

Mike of course realises Dee knows the real version, and that she only pursues it as entertainment, and to get her pound of flesh.

Dee was in the kitchen as Mike appeared downstairs; while young Annie is down the garden in the sun but looking herself not so sunny as she scans the ground beyond their fence.

Her young day always starts down her garden with Baskerville. She talks to him and quizzes him about where he went in the night and what he saw; did he talk with other cats, was there any word of Bob... but like most days, Baskin jumps around and skips across to have his chin tickled, or dances after thistledown...

...He never has a lot to say.

"Oh Baskin... surely there was some stray cat who has been speaking to the ghostly moon, or owl who's flapped across the woods and railway lines... or podgy pug whose owners take him everywhere and who knows where that high tower in the city is?"

Our Annie doesn't know that Baskin has no thought or image of his brother cat; no heart of loss or memory that nags of how it was, like Annie has. Of course or a dessert. She brightens as she feels a thought, or space to think, or is it just the shape of new departure in her search?

Why is there suddenly a buzzing from the house? Annie spins around and Baskin thinks she is going to throw something for him that he will chase after.

She looks up towards the house where two faces are conversing in profile then both turn to glance down the garden to her. Seeing she has spotted them Mike lifts his face to catch her eye; he's grinning as he waves to call her up; Dee though, still looks mystified as he has only so far said he's got a vague new lead and wants them both to come and chew it over with him.

Annie's on her way back up, and Baskin trotting like a demon furry toy his tail stuck up and quivered like a horse whip at the top; till seeing she is heading in veers off to shoot up fence post.

Inside Annie is greeted by Dee's,

"just doing you some toast love…"

and Michael's

"Any new clues today babe?"

At which she pulls her thoughts in, reads them, and says as if only just then finding where they lead:

"Well funny Dad, but no… and maybe yes as well. There's nothing out there in the garden really, I've looked around but it's really fairly cold… yeah but, hmm… while I was trying to see if Basky found anything in the night…"

And it must be said here that Dee and Michael are by this time well used to their daughter bringing in reports of 'nothing useful from the hedgehogs etc.'

From which they do not fear for their daughter's sanity because she makes it seem so mundane and matter of fact when she's telling it; but they share no detail of her exchanges with neighbours or grandparents.

Annie has found her mental image and continues:

"...Yes Baskin seems pretty useless these days, but after I was seeing what he had found out... well, I suppose just after seeing that as usual he was no help at all... just then it arrived with me that there was something new in the air, but it... it seemed to feel as if somehow it was concealed, or at least like a part of it in some way by someone; you know... they knew it but were keeping it to themselves for some reason!"

Mike looks sideways at Dee and thinks about the newspaper he has got tucked away to show them. He asks himself what sort of a little psychic monster they have managed to create; and thinking of course that the rather weird side of Annie must be from Dee's genes.

So while he's got them both there and paying attention he reaches up to the kitchen cupboard door where he had tucked the paper as he came in last night.

Mike rustles through the paper looking for the page and picture. On finding it he holds it closed on finger and intones scanning both female faces with a look of serious resolve to not be swayed:

"Right, and just before I start, none of what I'm going to show you can be used as an excuse to think we can drop everything and go waltzing off at vast expense to who knows where on some wild goose chase okay?

What I've got is probably nothing but I brought it home anyway because I thought you both would like..."

"... Oh for crying out loud Michael Sparks, are you going to prattle on for the rest of the day or are you going to give us some idea what this is all about!"

And brought to a halt mid flow he draws his horns in and

fumbles to open the paper at them.

"Okay now girls, and don't go getting too excited about all this, just have a look and enjoy the fact that it might remind you a bit of something… even if there's no connection."

"Just get on with it!"

He spreads the page and holds it up to them.

"Hey Dad it's Bobcat isn't it… is it from round here?"

"I thought it looked like him too love, though I know it cannot really be him."

"It is Dad… and that's the woman I told you about that night, yes and I can see now that it's up on the same tower too!"

Mike is not entirely surprised at Annie's certainty, though he cannot for his life think how his little girl could possibly have seen her cat up a tower from a couple of hundred miles away.

He cannot even start to picture what this gift of sight can really be; he wonders with some consternation if it includes the ability to dream her way through bedroom walls in the night when they assume she is just peacefully asleep and out of it.

Then Dee who was quickly scanning over the paper and story says quickly before Annie starts to implore them to take her to Paris,

"But as Dad has said love, it is both too far, and far too expensive for us all to just go shooting off there to search for him."

"I know Mum… but it wouldn't do us much good if we did, Bobby's not in that country now anyway. Though it may well help us if we ring the paper to see if they have the name and address of the woman."

"Well yes… of course that was going to be my next step Annie, if we thought it looked like him!"

Mike lies… and smarting inwardly to see his daughter is a step ahead of him… again!

Chapter Twenty

Mushrooms

Crunch, scrunch… and finally, munch.

A mouse's head gives little more than a stifled squeak that terminates as final thoughts shut down when Bobcat rips it off with a twist of his jaw; and grins as fangs cut in like man in Sushi bar devouring raw fish and slurping wine, and smiling at girls who show him what if the fates were kind his life might have been… for him now as his sun sinks low, a little late perhaps.

But not too late for Bobcat, this is all just now he wants from life; a munchy mouse, and the final dying embers of an evening sky to draw his nose west.

For two nights when his new mum brought him home he stayed living in their caravan on the drive. Ken blocked the door a few inches open with a log and a chain and padlock, so Bob… or Blackjack as he is to them, would have the freedom of their garden in the night.

It took some persuasion from Ken to get Ronnie to put a notice up on the lost and found board in the village.

Yesterday the entire Sparks family drove through the village in their van on their way home from Granny's house; they went within ten yards of it, but also in the middle of an argument about who was the best dancer at the holiday camp last year. Annie reckons that their family possesses six feet, but five of them are left feet! (guess which ones) Mike says there are four left feet among the six, but so he doesn't get one or other woman going at him he has not revealed which one of them it is. Of course he's bound to count himself as having one of each.

But past and on they went towards their home to be greeted by a very hungry yowling Baskerville.

If they had known that the cat they have searched for and that has been to France and back, was just a few yards away up a quiet road that they went past… well… well I suppose they would have turned round and gone back!

The first couple of days home for Bob a warm front moved in and obliterated any beckoning orange glow in his western sky. But tonight the rain is through, and strata-cumulous that vaporised and thinned out as evening came on, then lit itself and flamed across the orange ceiling.

That first night home rain rattled like buck-shot on the caravan's roof, so Bobcat only popped out just the once to have a wee beneath; down below he crouched with darting eyes and the smell of flicked road tar and the lingering dust of French cobblestones.

He stayed there to sniff out from below at the night, and see if it said what to do; it said jump back inside above to munch some bickies and lap some water… and get your head down again.

Bob did, and having done it seemed as well to stay that way; and soon another lazy day crept pleasantly through.

Tonight the golden sky went dull and dark, and where it fell, the stars rose up in spangled patterned image just as this on other nights.

Four feet begin their trepidacious search as if they set off on thin ice, or on a hot tin roof perhaps; and so beget an anxious yowl as caravan is left behind.

Passing the last few gardens a lane is crossed. Through thorny hedge to dewy field as clear sky draws the warmth away to space, and spores of mushrooms feel the freshness on their minute heads and parachute down between the tree-like stems of blades of grass to wiggle their tiny toes into the wormy soil.

A big old field-mushroom from a few nights back has a meaty smell like tinned cat food, and stops Bob in his tracks to sniff… if he were ravenous it might be worth a bite, but not yet, not tonight.

Tonight a sudden rustle back in hedge is followed by a squeak as mouse finds other mouse has queered his pitch, now backed up against a clump of oxlips and seeming determined to loiter if he can.

Such all consuming things like this ask all your concentration as you defend your claim and get to work to oust the infiltrator. In your short life you've never even seen a cat; even if you had what are the chances of one turning up in the middle of nowhere as you go about your rightful business of eviction.

Then as we said at the start… crunch, scrunch… and finally munch… Let's hope he had a couple of months to pass his genes on.

A small yet fairly deep valley starts where a scruffy copse of hazel and hornbeam lolls on its rim, and slopes as if to fall into its depth; but as it does so going thin where lack of topsoil leaves so many roots exposed.

Bobcat winds his way beneath the thinning measly trees and pads across the mossy leaf mould pungent soil; and almost down he goes below a fence quite new that says its owners think from here on it can count as field; though never quite after their initial enthusiasm for having a horse and their own field, got back to cutting down the thinning weedy trees beyond.

Sure enough, after a few more yards trees cease, and Bobcat finds the proper open grass that the people always thought would be an inexhaustible expanse of lush greenness for Diamond. It has taken her just nine months to have it nibbled bare; now it's poached and soggy because the little valley's so deep and narrow that except in mid summer it hardly ever gets the sun.

The dear old horse is rarely brought the saddle now, she's really just the plodding memory of a cantering dream that they once had.

To Bobcat it is just another field that he must cross, and having horse he'll watch to see if head lifts or the ears go back. A clattered snort of breath through nose curtailed by rather lonely whinny sounds okay, and Bobcat points his own nose west.

Halfway over his instincts search with ears cocked as the field evokes the memory of barking baying dogs that echoed through the trees that day near Railway Wood; that growing nearer sent his little legs like frantic windmills flailing out to gain the safety of the trees. Yes that day that nearly was his last has left him careful when he goes across all open spaces.

'Halted in moonlight here today,

With one paw raised, and two ears cocked,

No howling banshees haunt the dell, nor cannon' murderous from the wood beyond.

This night breathes peace, and fungous fume,

With scent of flowers sunk and soaked in aqueous dew, and velvet gloom,

Where mist and moonlight make a veil for stars to wink through;

Where settled safety coolly shines and lights his path,

Then a distant dog that hears or smells some passing mangy fox howls out... and makes him duck!'

A precautionary trot brings him more quickly through the haunting flares of no-man's-land, where if panic strikes he might waste precious moments seeing where to flee to get through nearest fence.

One hour on, the old horse stands out in moonlight like stone, but breathing steam... with scant memory that a little cat walked through her lonely misty field... Then as a badger trundles past, and after that when later still a fox with cubs, she will not know a cat was there...

...Though someone knows; someone who though peacefully asleep, is watchful. Annie follows... or is it more, floats fitfully after, in the turbulence of her dreams. Suspended depths of layered thought make watching at close quarters fraught, and problematic; and she finds she keeps on sliding back to her day at school and playing ball with a particular girl at break time; and each time she throws ball shouts 'you keep it now' but back it comes again! She knows she needs to be elsewhere but isn't quite awake enou... or is it not asleep enough to focus clearly.

Now Bobcat is on a hill with steady rise and a long climb dragging up makes him seek water, which he finds. So crouched to lap from puddle beneath a tap on the corner of an outlying barn he also sees a stack of hay bales looking somewhat like a welcome bed for a weary little Manx cat.

You tiptoe in and sniff for threat of dogs who scout around, or maybe even sleep here sometimes; all these informations must be sought; happily it smells just of summer fields, and summer nights, and somewhere to lay your hat… which you do not have, and even mice.

He hoicks himself up bale by bale to get safe height, and extra seconds if while sleeping, passing dog gets wind of him and makes an ambush.

Pushing round and round among now scruffy bales of hay not needed to feed the farmer's cattle last winter; as he relaxes sniffing the warm fermenting breath of last years harvest, he flops down with rewarded sigh.

Bobcat sinks through crimson gloom to darkness as his breathing settles for what's left of the night.

And in the end you even hear the gentle rattle of a purr.

Chapter Twenty-One

A Few Days On

Yes a few days on, with comfy barn of hay bales far behind his little stumpy tail.

He's even made a fair few miles in daylight in the preceding twenty-four hours, and has kept going west fairly well, though the weather hasn't helped much. We have a tropical maritime air-stream sliding over England, that means mild and moist and very pleasant to get about; but it also means that with it being overcast, except by feeling which side the wind is coming from and trying to keep it that way, there is really no other sense to tell you if you're not just going round in big circles as you push through woods and wild spaces.

Bobcat to be fair has done pretty well at keeping straight; he's quite the seasoned traveller now. He did spend half a day veering more and more to the north but by the time it was dark the bank of the River Medway made him choose to either turn or swim, so stopped him going that way; it was like he heard a voice, or felt a voice that called him left… at any rate that's where he went.

Unspecific and uncounted the hours pass; he seems to be keeping this river in sight most of the time and it leads him like an amiable meandering snake.

In the morning while that first thin stream of milky light just trickles through the tops of clouds, and reaching ground then tickles whiskered celandines; where ferns are poised and moisture hung... 'and treetops stand dark against the stars grown pale, then clear and shrill a distant farm-cock crows... and there's a wall of mist along the vale, where willows shake their watery sounding leaves'...

...he's found a little bay between two willow trees where the bank is broken down and the earth and turf leading into the water is all stodged and poached by the hooves of the cattle that come down there to drink.

He finds a puddle in a hoof print so he doesn't even have to lean out over the sweeping dark waters of the river.

This all feels that life has taken on and settled to a natural slant, of water, food, fine weather and warm dry barns to sleep in. He does not picture winter, but no doubt being Bobcat, if he is still out here when it arrives he will just happen to amble through the garden of a nice woman with a kind heart and a warm house, and a frequently open door; but if that does happen, it is unlikely that as 'spring brings back blue days and fair', he will still remember where he was meant to be going.

That's enough water drunk from the hoof print puddle. Looking up your cats' eyes focus on the reeds in front of you, where nothing moves... and if that 'nothing' were to remain motionless and still not move for a few more seconds you would have looked away and straightened up and stretched and headed on; but stretching cats look just like cats about to spring, and coot who could have kept her head down explodes from reeds and flaps and flails and races over surface to the other bank.

Her clutch of startled dozing chicks below her downy breast find Mum has gone and poke their heads above the parapet to snuff the air, and to see what's what with all this sudden stuff.

Bobcat thinks... as best as Bobcat can... that there's a sudden dinner spread in front of him, and all he needs is knife and fork. Though he'll make do with teeth and claws for now.

Then two leap east and two go west, and one goes out the back but the last one, and perhaps not the brightest candle in the church is so startled by the others' exits that she loses her head and jumps straight into Bobcat's grateful arms… and looses her head a second time!

Happily he munches his free hot dinner, alternately tearing off mouthfuls then flicking his head about to jettison feathers. At the end of his meal this quiet water hole looks like someone has taken apart an old feather pillow.

Meal over he has another drink to wash it down and clean his chops, so he can sniff what's what as he goes on… and won't smell to other predators like he's carrying a fresh kill with him.

With tummy full of hot coot he probably won't go far now because it brings on that warm glow. Whenever a cat is walking it is hunting too, but having eaten no doubt he'll lie down quite soon.

A hundred yards along the bank a tree that fell in the Great Storm still lies there dead and rotting, half in water and half on land with its trunk all hollowed out by age, but mostly dry inside.

Bobcat spots this natural doorway and sneaks down the bank for a closer sniff; it seems not to be anyone's lodgings so he tiptoes in. Again that meaty smell of fungus lifts his nose, and there are many stuck twigs lodged here and there from when the winter river floods and rises and much that drags along the bank comes pushing in.

But all that's pushing in today has found a comfy hollowed corner to curl up in. He only needs to go round once and then flops down like a cowpat landing behind a cow… and a similar colour!

What are his dreams… there's none to say; or close enough to see if whiskers twitch we do not stay.

Later refreshed and drawn to move again he emerges and the sun is properly up. Back up the bank he points his nose along the field that became dewy when the sky cleared in the night, and is still dewy but drying quickly in the early climbing sun.

Now his food has gone down it is easy to make a little more speed, and sometimes almost breaks into a trot.

A hedge comes up he's through and then another field, with long grass grown for a hay crop here so his horizons shrink; and always he is wary for the howl of dogs.

After a small copse there are no fields for a while, just trees on little slopes with gorse and broom all yellow flowered, and when the day gets warm will scent the air so pungently your head will swim.

He presses on until a sudden path goes off to left… he stops, though not sure why. He does not know this path, yet something seems to make him think it is his way and he looks along and sniffs the air for answers.

Nothing from the tepid air assures his thought, but it's as if a voice he knows is somewhere there ahead of him… and so he goes.

Chapter Twenty-Two

Nearly There

"Wakey wakey sleeping beauty, it's time to let your eye lids flutter open at the tender kiss of Prince Charming…"

Dee calls out as she climbs the stairs to get her daughter up for school. At top step turns on landing leans to open door and hears her daughter,

"I've been awake and sitting up for a little while Mum… I think we'll find him soon."

As Dee comes in indeed she finds her daughter sitting up in bed awake; perhaps awake but deep it seems in thought, or in her mind part somewhere else.

And Annie smiles with confidence as though there's no longer need to sketch the safe landscape of doubt into her picture. She looks as if right now all the shapes and colours are falling into place for her.

"I think he's somewhere that we know…

That far off sunny day some time ago, we walked to a river down some little path,

Where Daddy slipped, and slid, and bumped right down a muddy slope and we both laughed,

But he jumped up and shouted, 'how would we fancy sliding over roots and stuff on our bums?',

So we said it looked fun,

And he just sulked…

Where were we then Mum; it was on the way down to that big slow river wasn't it?"

"Yes of course it was love… well, it will have seemed quite a big river to you then I suppose, though it's not that wide really. So, what was it that you saw down there in your dream Annie?"

"Bobcat's somewhere down there now Mum… I managed to find him a couple of times in the night; I was with him again just before I woke up too. I think he is on his way to our old house; well it must be to our old home, because there is nowhere else he could be trying to find round there, is there?"

"Well if you are right, I'm sure we'll soon know."

"Yes, we can be there to meet him can't we Mum?"

"Oh that's a bit difficult love, we must go to school… yes and Dad's doing a late shift today so we can't get there till tomorrow at the earliest. No, I was saying that I meant that we will know because the new people have been sending mail on to us and can easily find our number... or the landlord of the flats will get hold of us for them if they ask him."

Though Dee knows they will all have to make an expedition to their old house to see if he is really there; it is out of the question not to respond to the desire of their daughter to find her cat... or at least to help her know if her dream was just mistaken.

"I'm scared that if we can't get there to meet him he might wander off the next day! No... no, I suppose he has only got there because he thinks it's his home, so that's where he will try to stay when he finds it."

Dee is rummaging through Annie's draws to choose her school things for the day, and has to wait to ask if she's got PE.

Their day slides in, and time slides on, with bits that fit and bits that don't, and some that when you shove and wiggle do the job... but just as any other day, it goes.

Then walking home with Catherine later, Annie wants to take the opportunity to clear her thoughts and frustrations about finally thinking she knows where her cat is, and maybe getting her little friend home at last.

"So go on then Annie Sparks, I can see you're tingling inside with something... hey, you're not pregnant are you? It's okay I'm only joking mate! (Annie may think she is a pretty hot kisser but though she has youthful sexy daydreams, she has never even thought that she might ever go any further with any boy) Come on then, you wanted to tell me earlier about the latest stuff with Bobcat?"

"Well okay Cat… you see it's all made so much more difficult because I can't go off to look for him on my own. One night I reckon I knew exactly where he was; when it woke me up I found myself downstairs in our hall fumbling in the key dish for Dad's van keys."

"So do you reckon you could drive it if you had to?"

"I sat in the driver's seat with Dad there as well one day, and I couldn't even reach the pedals… but of course in the dream I was sure I would suddenly be able to do it.

"It is so frustrating not being able to get myself around to look for Bobby. I know it's hard for Mum and Dad too; they want to help me in my search, though really they don't believe he will ever be found."

"Have they said that Annie?"

"No of course not, they are really nice about it all the time… but I've felt what they're thinking lots of times, and it's mostly just something they go along with to make me happy; well except that they also think it has been a good thing for making us all more close too… yes and lots of times they reckon our little expeditions have been good fun, and educational as well, Dad reckoned once or twice."

"Why don't you put your mum and dad on the spot one

day and ask them if they still believe you're going to find Bobcat eventually. If they sit you gently down and say 'sorry Annie, we think he's gone forever now', you'll know it's down to you to accept it or go it alone."

"Yes but it would mean going it completely alone wouldn't it? I could hardly still expect them to drive me around after they have been made to admit they think he's gone forever could I Cat?"

"I s'pose not… but maybe they are right, maybe your dreams are… just dreams Annie?"

"On the surface you could think that… but underneath, no Cat… no it's not like that… When they happen, I come out of whatever I'm dreaming and I know I'm seeing something that is really there.
"Yes, okay, like what about The Eiffel Tower? A week later there's a picture of what I saw in a newspaper; I mean, I don't need to be convinced that what I see at night is real, but if I was in doubt that would have shown me the truth wouldn't it?"

"Yeah, that's true enough I suppose Annie. But hang on… so why didn't that newspaper article convince your mum and dad it's all real then?"

"Because they think I have an unusual ability to see what's coming; so that I somehow guessed there would be a black cat taken up the Eiffel Tower… least that's what it felt like with that one."

"Right I see Annie… I think; anyway, the important thing is are they going to take you back to your old house to see if he's there?

"Oh yes Cat, Mum's quite happy to do that, it's just that Dad is doing a late shift on overtime today so it will be tomorrow at the earliest.

"You see, I think of Bobcat just waiting there for us to come, with no food and nothing to do for two days, but of course it isn't really like that for him, it's just what he's been doing for the last eight weeks.

"And at first I was thinking he might find us not there and wander on the same day he gets there; but of course he will try and stay there because he still thinks it's his home."

"So Annie, perhaps at long last you are about to get your cat back!

"But imagine if you get over there and find that all your dreams have been just… well, just dreams."

"Oh don't Cat, it doesn't bear thinking about does it; I would never be able to look Mum and Dad in the face again would I?"

Later as the throstle sings his evening tune, and throws his brittle rebuke to any challengers across the softened air, and higher up the martins zip and glide as if on glass, and higher even still are swifts who will fade up into the gloaming blue to spend their dozed night floating on transparent beds of marbled nitrogen; while this brings on the night a little cat will make his way along a path away from river meadows up a windy way and into woods.

'Further up he intersects a little stream and has to jump from stone to stone,

And though he cannot read the words cut deep into the silvered bark of tree, 'Darren' then a heart, then 'Alice', still attests that a Canadian soldier billeted in the mansion house in the second war, shared love with a woman from the village here.

Did they make it back to Alberta to have a family and grow old together?

Do they sit together as we speak?

Who knows, or from then who can say...

Which of them carved these words?

This tree just says that there was love... at least one way.'

This gurgled stream recedes behind as Bobcat scrambles up the slope; nor does he see the gouged heart and names that hang forlorn and still defiant under years of lichen and the assault of sun and frost.

He sees an unfamiliar path where bracken fringes on the left, where heather almost gets a toe-hold then defers to broom and gorse; tall silvered silver birches host ravenous bracket fungi who ten years on will bring them down to moulder in the tangled growth on dingy slope.

Seeing these there is for him no fond recognition of somewhere he often went, as he never came this way.

Passing a clump of gorse and broom, the pungent yellow flowers scent the air, and mean you taste the breeze as much as feel its urgent stroking... so why if this and these scents are known to him and not unique to here and now; why has he just stopped with both ears cocked and one paw raised... and one nose, well his only nose poked high and waffling to confirm a connection?

> *'The light is failing fast and soon*
> *The flutuous owl will haunt and warble through the dell,*
> *And all who seek their food in dark*
> *Will pop from holes, or slide down trees, or slither through wet grass away from pond and pool.'*

Bobcat still with one paw raised has spotted (with his nose) the unique aroma of a bulk tank being flushed out ready for the morning milking... Unique because it is the sweet fatty milk of a milking herd of ewes that spills its scent onto the waft of gloaming; nothing else could smell like this, least not in this corner of Kent; it is the only milking herd of ewes for many miles.

The one raised paw to floor goes down to take another step, almost with resignation it appears; there seems no relish in the padding paws that follow on; it's more like he is summoned home for bed or something arduous, or maybe even that's better shunned if possible.

And step and step and step goes paw by paw; the path will take him out of line of scent quite soon, but though he doesn't know it with his conscious mind two giant wellingtonias poke head and shoulders from the skyline and are imprinted in his memory like the eyes of his mother.

It takes longer than you might think to skirt a field when you are almost reluctant to get home... when field mice fizz and rustle in the sprouting shiny wheat... When you remember being called by Dee from distant house and gambling home to find your chops are prized apart and a socking great worm pill shoved down.

So when life's good you drag it out, you sniff and pounce and make the most of all you find.

It is almost with astonishment you push through hedge and stare across a lane at gates... where you were some time, who knows how long before. That you were here is certain though, nor feels it something that you need to doubt; it's just your drive, your shrubs, your grass and trees... and background outline of your mansion-house and stable block.

He wanders up into the orchard where tired trees un-pruned for years show blossom but will yield scarce one basket of apples each. And those will fall in the main unpicked, all wasp-munched and worm burrowed.

It is nearly dark and a barn owl swerves and flaps through trees on wings soft like a giant white moth, but not seeking for night flower nectar.

Bobcat wary crouches darkly till he's gone.

Now olive shiny leaves moon glazed and flowers hung with luminescence line the rhododendron way; and make his familiar path past garages to an old archway and a cobbled courtyard.

Through archway you bear right to reach the glass door of your porch, which is always blocked permanently open to give you and your adopted brother access to and from the woodshed through each night.

It is with some surprise, and a certain halting disconsolation that you find the door closed against you; eagerly sniffing for clues and the scent of your people, you find nothing that you would have expected to find... not waft of Dee's garden anorak, nor pungent fume of Michael's boots... or even from inside the door the crunchy smell from bowl of night time's china clattered shake of munchies.

Smells do come out but none you know so you sit back

perplexed and for this moment somewhat thwarted.

Bobcat turns to scout around his courtyard; there the peeling paint of stable doors and mower shed, and gutters glowing gilded by the moon.

In the corner is his opening through to dewy garden where any moment Baskerville would usually come dancing through with squeaking mouse in mouth to drop and look away, letting it run a pace or two, but as radar ears anticipate and monitor the futile bid for freedom then he springs again.

Baskerville has not appeared. The courtyard is Bobcat's, and as far we can see… only Bobcat's. He wants these missing bits to slot into place now; the novelty of just being back in his real home is already wearing thin.

In the absence of these missing links you feel bereft; like time has played some rouse on you, or holding back some vital clue, or rotten fate has snuck its concealing foot over the vital dropped piece of jigsaw that you need to have to make the scene come true.

Now in centre of the yard, and starlight twinkles in the dome of inky blackness; Bobcat waits for the right trigger or signal to land in his lap.

What then arrives is more in the form of a voice… no, not quite a voice, more the feeling of a thought, but not his own; no not his own for his thoughts are silent and stranded in the gardens of his hope.

These words are not like from his people, where you know the phases of your day that their utterances relate to; no these speak far more directly to your cat mind.

Bobcat feels a dreamy "hello to you" arrive, and pauses sniffing scented air. He knows these thoughts come from another cat and he would bristle to do battle if there were even the faintest hint of attitude or rivalry in their tone; but they were calm, almost detached.

Bob glances up and down but nothing finds, not Baskerville nor passing stray. Again the owl gives haunted screech as it goes out across the fields.

"Hello to you my brother cat, have you come far?"

Bob knows that yes, he's come so far to be here where his people and his own brother cat should be; yet now it is uncertain just where he was before he set out.

Searching round his eye is drawn to source of words; there beneath the old rusting car that he and Baskerville took shelter under on the night of the great storm… there two luminous green eyes stare soulfully out across the cobbled yard… a moment's hope that it might be… but no, it's not his adopted brother; the poise is languid and has none of Baskin's urgency… and something speaks of permanence.

Bob feels his own question:

"How long have you been here, what brings you here today? I live here but have never seen you here before…"

The green eyes dream back to him:

"Yes I am here… I was left here so long ago. I lived up in the loft over that stable with my man. I don't know where he went but I am waiting still for his return.

"I remember you were here playing in the sun with your brother when you were just kittens. Yes, and I knew you in this dark some years ago when the winds howled round the courtyard and you came in here beside me for a while… but did not see me here.

"My man went through that archway there… a while ago, I am not sure just how long. I knew I should expect it to be a long time because he fussed my head and looked back many times as he went down the road… I think perhaps it will be soon."

"My man went through that archway there… a while ago,

"Yes I'm a little lost as well; this is my proper home but I was taken somewhere with my people, but I liked to be with them here so I came back to find them. This is certainly the place we always were, but now…"

Disraeli has known many other cats come and go here… and no doubt will see many more.

"It seems that we have much to share my friend; we can wait together if you like… come under this old cart with me it's dry and warm here."

Chapter Twenty-Three

Her Day Arrives

"Just stay exactly as you are Bobby, don't go running off anywhere please. I can't wake Mum and Dad yet, it's still too early."

Annie is half awake… or is she half asleep? It's always open to debate, 'awake, asleep'? That state where each fails glumly to achieve domination… and some might call it one and some the other; whichever it be her nimble thoughts work hard comparing options and trading hope against the odds on disappointment… like a pessimistic gambler.

It's scarcely six o'clock and dad's done overtime so the rule is he must be left to snore until he's snored enough…

"Oh Christ Dad, you could snore for England, and how does Mum manage to sleep through it? I suppose by answering… or arguing with her little wheezy ones."

Annie listens impatiently from her bed in the next room, feeling as in other years like her younger self waiting for Mum and Dad to wake on Christmas day; then with a sigh she sinks through crimson gloom and lets herself drift off again, and adds her tiny snuffles to the glorious choir of hogs.

While she dozes a myriad colours and scenes flicker and fade across and through her thought, though she cannot focus or settle on any single scene; but again she sees her cat wandering away that first night when he ended up sleeping in Jan Gordon's garden shed, and Biff the bloodhound sniffed him out in the morning and gave him a rude awakening...

And the railway where its hard shiny rails were running through the wood, and once again feels herself urging him to get across before the train comes clattering round the bend...

She was on her way to school and so awake and not properly with him when Bob was chased across that field by dogs and only made it up his tree as they were snapping at his desperate heels; but her distant thoughts were with him nevertheless...

After weeks in the housing estates and streets of suburbia she saw him taken across the sea and was barely asleep one night when she found he was at the top of a huge tower and in the arms of a strange woman!

When Annie saw him home in England she knew more certainly there was a chance of seeing him again...

When she saw he had left his nest in Ken and Ronnie's caravan, though she had no real idea where it was Annie believed it would be only a matter of time till he would reach his journey's end and she would have her chance to get him back.

Now here she lies this small but growing girl, who only partially asleep feels countdown start to what she seeks.

An hour slides... the sun its nightly semi-circumnavigation of the globe complete climbs warmly in the sky again. Her distant cat has wandered out when he heard the porch door of the flat open. Two hours ago Vernon Smith came on his milk round from Palmers Farm, but Bobcat stayed out of sight because he remembered and didn't like the diesel van's smell, and its chug and throb.

Then when the porch door opened he thought this would finally be Dee come out to get him so he trotted forth with a welcoming clucking meow… but it was some other woman. She was friendly enough, and crouched to stroke his head and tickle his chin; and when she stood up with her milk he nearly followed her inside, but the strange smells that wafted down the stairs confused him. He stayed outside.

As Janice gets back upstairs into the flat with their milk she tells her man about the funny little cat out in the courtyard:

"It's weird Tel, he seems to be waiting out there."

"So how do you know he isn't just admiring the view… or enjoying the morning sun?"

"Well, I suppose because he liked attention… but didn't seem to want anything. I mean, he ran to see me as I came out as if he thought he knew me, or at least expected to know me."

"Perhaps he's just with people who have moved into one of the flats in the big house and he's been shoved outside to have a look around… yeah, or just to go for a crap in the garden!"

"I suppose it could just be that but he just looks as if he thinks this is where he is meant to be.

"Hey Tel… what about the last people? Well, I mean they had a cat didn't they; we saw it when they let us have a look round the flat that day… or was it two cats even."

"Yeah so it can't be one of them because they said they were moving miles away Babe."

"Yes but what if the cat had set off back more or less as soon as they got to their new place; that would have given him… well, weeks and weeks to get here."

"Well you've seen him love, did he look much like either of their cats… I'm afraid that to me all cats look much the same."

"Yes me too really; I was so keen to see the view of the gardens etc when we came here that day that I hardly looked at the cats. I remember the girl, she was really sweet and a bright cheeky little thing; she told us more about everything than her mum and dad and they seemed almost a little bit in awe of her Tel?"

"Yeah I picked that up as well love. That's right, and she said some really off the wall things when she took me for a guided tour of the gardens. I remember thinking it was a shame we wouldn't be having them as neighbours… yeah and her mum was a tidy bit of kit as well!"

"I knew you'd be getting that in, you dribbled enough when we were looking round the place!

"But seriously Tel, do you think I should try to get in touch with them just in case?"

"Maybe, except that cats often go astray when people move.

What if they have lost one but it's not this one... they'll come dashing round with their little girl all happy and only to find that it's someone else's; was there really nothing that would mark it as the real thing... I don't know, perhaps a wooden leg or something!"

"When was the last time you saw a cat with a wooden leg Tel? Hang on though I've just realised... it didn't have a wooden leg, but I reckon it was a... what are those cats called that have no tail?"

"Hmm, a bit careless with car doors perhaps?"

"No you tosser, there's a breed from somewhere in Britain that grows like that. Anyway love, this one is like that. Hey, why don't you go out to take a look and see if he's still there?"

"Well just let me finish my naffing cornflakes and I'll take my coffee out in the sun with me to have a look."

Five miles away someone else is taking a look. That picture and caption of a cat up the Eiffel Tower that Allan brought to work to show Michael Sparks... Ronnie now has a copy too. She sits on the front step of their nice comfy bungalow in the sun, and smiling at the memory of her escapade at the top of the Eiffel Tower with her furry friend.

Looking at the image of herself and Blackjack, and with the knobbly carpet of Paris laid out below, she tries hard to imagine where he is today. Perhaps when he wandered away he found a family down in the village who took him in to be doted on by all the... children? This thought does not slide lightly from her mind, of families, children etc; it pulls a pool of coolness like the wind behind an underground train, and leaving Ronnie hollowed out and searching her emptiness for a warm thought.

"Have his own people seen the picture yet?"

This sudden thought has quivered her lips but is not quite speaking through them. If Blackjack's people have seen the picture did they think for even one minute that it could be their cat all those miles away… yes and miles above the ground as well! Veronica was clutching him so tightly, and he was so wrapped up in her arms that you would have to guess if he had a tail or not.

The breeze that had just made Veronica shiver a little where a growing morning cloud bulges with light and covers the sun for a while, now having passed, the warmth and stillness settles around her.

A waft of scent and pollen from summer bedding plants fertilises her thought, if not her eggs!

"I wonder if I should be doing anything else to help them find their cat… but do they want to find him? Lots of people don't like their animals and are relieved when they take a walk… No, I can see that was not the case, Blackjack was so personable and so much loved attention; there's little doubt in my mind that he came from a family who adored him.

"So what else should I have done? I guess that notice in the village was unlikely to unearth them unless they lived in or near the village themselves… or if a friend of theirs saw it perhaps. Still, no one called me about it so that was that.

"Hey now! What about a call to the paper who did the

article… if they did see it and called the paper to ask about the cat they may have left their address or something."

(In fact Dee did call the paper to try and get in touch with the woman in the photograph. She learned that the journalist was unable to get their details because they feared some form of admonishment from the French authorities. But Dee left her own details at the paper.)

"I would so love to know if that little cat ever makes it home. That he was with me for a while makes me feel responsible for the subsequent disappearance from his lodgings in our caravan.

If only I had put my foot down and insisted we have him in the house… I don't know though, Ken reckoned Blackjack had it in his mind to be somewhere, and it did seem like that.

"I suppose there's no point contacting the paper? Yes that actually seems like the next thing I should do. His people just might have seen it and called in the last few days.

"It could be my task for this morning, and I would feel I had done all that's come to mind so far to see what became of him. Yes and won't it be nice to be told that he's safe at home with his people again."

Veronica is resolved to pursue the paper straight after breakfast, and she does. And yes, they do give her the details of the Sparks family, so some of the pieces of the jigsaw are falling into place.

People are easy to find, she thinks to herself as she lets their phone ring one more ring before giving up with a resolve to try again later. She muses to herself that finding one little black Manx cat in the middle of who knows where could

207

remain the missing piece of the jigsaw. The Sparks family may have to content themselves with at least knowing the details of his sojourn in France.

If Ronnie knew even the slightest thing about little Annie Sparks, she would know that Annie will be doing anything but contenting herself with only hearing about her cat's sojourn in France.

As we speak she is clambering into the back of her dad's van after an exhausting hour cajoling and nagging her mum and dad to get their skates on and get moving.

"Come on Mum we haven't got all day!"

Dee, though still a little numb between the ears this early in the day so correspondingly crabby, still resists the desire to rebuke her eager daughter… after all it sort of is her day and had been promised to her.

"Okay love, I had to check the cupboard to see what food we need for tonight… then I spotted half a mouse that Baskerville must have left a few days ago behind the ironing board.

"I had thought there seemed a bit of a whiff in the kitchen lately; I presumed it was just something to do with your dad."

"Oy, I heard that!"

But Annie was more distracted by the shopping angle:

"But why do you need to know what food we've got now Mum?"

"Well if Bobcat isn't there, we will just go straight to the supermarket before it gets too crowded love."

"What do you mean 'if he isn't there', I've seen him with my own... well, sort of eyes."

"But if we find him, of course we'll bring him straight home again love, and leave you and Dad at home with him. Anyway, we're on our way now so what will be will be."

Dee waits until Mike starts the van before announcing that like in every American movie where a family are going somewhere in a car, she feels singing might help to stimulate her loins and get her arse into gear, and so launches into something volatile and sexy from the Bizet's opera Carmen, and also fondling Mike where Annie from behind the seat cannot see, but to ensure he approves of her artistry.

Her song done... or words run out of, and the miles starting to notch up, Dee turns to Annie in the back to ask her something, but Mike with the same intention shouts over his shoulder:

"If he's there Annie, do you think he'll remember us?"

"Yeah of course he will Dad... he'll probably just think we've all been out to the shops for rather a long time or something."

"You reckon he won't think he's been travelling for about two months then love?"

"I don't think his mind works like that. Each new day just comes along and he only kind of remembers the day before if something happens again from it that he finds he already knows."

"Okay I see… said the blind man to the dog that wasn't there!"

Mike intones quizzically.

"Don't waste your time explaining things to Dad Honey, it's like trying to teach algebra to a chicken! Don't worry, I know what you're saying."

Annie giggles and squeezes her mum's shoulder; then gives her dad's ribs a poke too in case he feels left out.

Miles further on they turn at a village green; 'The Greyhound' on the corner reminds them of times they all walked up the lane and across the rec in the dark, and how once, only as they reached the street-lights of the village glanced back and noticed one black and one black and white figure padding along a few yards behind. Mike, because he was frightened that if they all walked back with the cats, Dee would decide it would be too late to go back up again so therefore better get Annie into bed and he would have to forego his beer, he volunteered to trot back with the boys while the girls got the drinks in.

Tumbling aqueous memories from the meandering stream of those days come flooding out, or flooding back… undoubtedly they flood.

This pub they swing in past holds a fair smattering of

memories that was life for them... though just for then. Life goes on and wheels go round and distance stretches between what you were and what you've now become; and feelings that you might one day go back have a hollow ring if truth be told.

Till much further down wheels swing the nose between two gateless stone posts, and through previous years of habit they stay in low gear to ease themselves over the tenants' speed humps. The landlord's own drive to the other road didn't have these, and Mike always joked that it was to keep the serfs slow and remind them that by rights they should still be on foot.

This familiar grinding note and lurch of humps makes ears prick up and a nose to twitch. Into courtyard they arrive, and up and out from under car a lost little cat comes running.

"Shit!"

Is all Mike says, then bites his lip, but Annie is climbing over onto Dee and ready to exit like a parachutist from a plane. Her mouth is moving but as yet without sound, though soon there will be lots of it.

Dee agog makes nothing save a sort of squeal and panting almost sexily as if encountering a particularly proficient lover; but she's the first to find more than one word:

"That's really amaz... I mean I really honestly never thought for one moment he would be here Annie!"

"I know you didn't Mum but just let me out please."

This first two point seven seconds have brought them to a

halt in the middle of the courtyard… and the next one point three gets Annie out the door and running. Bobcat who was coming out to meet the for him wholly expected arrival of their van (as on any other day) has a moment of panic as the sprinter approaches, but footfall and voice mean only one thing… he is in the right place, and at the right time.

Bobcat has almost completely disappeared, been picked up and cuddled so tightly that it might be some old rag doll in her arms.

He is still trying to decide if he's been unusually good, or excessively bad;

Annie's present grip and scent are not in his mental library.

But he'll happily put up with it because he knows he's home…

…at last.

So that was how it finished… almost?

In The Days That Followed

A family of five again… two cats and three humans… if you count Mike, and all happy, though at first Baskerville seems to have mislaid the memory of his adopted brother and yowls suspiciously when Bob gets too near. Soon enough he remembers, or just gets to know him again, and the two of them are curled up together on their favourite chair.

Annie Sparks is as happy as a sand-boy; but just how much can you cuddle one cat before it starts to get fed up with it, or does he really comprehend he's been away?

She has a thought, and goes upstairs to her room. She finds an old yet hardly written in school exercise book, of which the original purpose has been long forgot.

Annie chooses a pencil and settles herself on the edge of her bed; then decides to do this properly and clears some space on her homework table. She leans over the first blank page with her spare arm crooked round to shield it from prying eyes; then realising you don't need to hide your work when you're at home she straightens up and chews the end of her pencil.

The pencil tastes like an echoey classroom on any summer's afternoon final period… and most likely a Friday. She almost expects to hear the voice of the teacher reprimanding her for dreaming, or for chewing her pencil, or for allowing her ear to listen out for the final bell; but then the clear image of what she is going to do returns.

She begins to write a title, crosses it out, and starts another; finally a third which has a bit of both in it. It starts out as, 'Bobcat's long Wander', then 'My Cat's Walkabout' then 'Bobcat's long Walk'.

"I think I will write a long poem that has all the things I think he did. Blimey, that sounds like hard work, what's going to rhyme with cat… except mat or fat, and he becomes less and less fat as it goes along; and 'mat' is only any use when he's indoors somewhere.

"Then best thing is for it to be a book, then I won't have to piddle about trying to make it rhyme!"

You may feel Annie's approach to art is rather staccato or clinical, but one thing is certain, that she wants to capture the essence of his temporary absence from her life; to represent and preserve while it is still all fresh, what it was like to have lived with him not being there.

Nine O'clock that evening when Annie is more or less asleep, and Dee is just about to head out the door to meet the girls in town, she is vaguely aware that the phone is ringing downstairs; it is picked up quickly by Dee and you can from upstairs make out sort of 'oh yes' and 'hmm, that's really kind'; and where long pauses for the caller's words to speak out finish with Dee's pretend laugh of exasperation and something like 'oh Bob's a little blighter', Annie knows so clear of whom they speak, though not whom speaks with Dee.

In the morning over breakfast:

"Someone called Veronica phoned us last night Annie; you sort of know of her already love, the Eiffel Tower etc?

"She tells me she was his adopted mum for a little while. She's making you a photo album of all she did with him in France… apparently she first found him as they were about to drive onto the Shuttle to go under the channel… Bob had sneaked into their caravan before they left their home. She's going to bring the album round to give you and tell you the full story when it's all finished in a day or so."

A few weeks on the newspaper runs a follow up story and reprints the picture taken up the Eiffel Tower, but this time the article has another title and a large feature about Annie and Bobcat.

The editor hears about Annie's account still in the writing and asks to see it when it's done.

A year later Annie has a regular page for youngsters that earns her more pocket-money than most kids ever get to dream of… an unusual girl, made of a lot more than just a few kids' dreams!

The Others Who Were There

Jan Gordon, the mother of Biff, also sees the story of Bobcat in the paper; she phones the editor and subsequently sends in an account of her own small appearance on the stage of his expedition.

And Biff the bloodhound and his new and much-adored kid-sister Nancy the tortoise-shell whom he would happily die for, get a mention too.

'Gallic Male' the French hunk, who regularly sits with a snack or a newspaper on that same bench or another nearby in the busy French street, sometimes remembers Ronnie: he will always see an English woman with shy but inquisitively parted lips that begin to mouth a thought but fear disclosure. With another week in the cement works done and his work overalls left in the changing-room locker, he lounges and muses while he eats a pastry. "Was she really speaking to me in the language of lurve, or was I imagining it?' Though his thoughts spoke in French of course. Or he wonders, was she just some bored and romantically inclined youngish English woman (he saw their GB sticker) with a flirtatious mind and a fertile eye seeking intrigue and mystique?

He will never know… He will never know, therefore we will never know. Veronica would have an answer if we could ask. Yes if there were time or reason to probe Veronica's thought then we too might know… not but there is. So off as ships into the night their unrequited love departs.

What of Alice the maid from the big house where Jake Jones worked before he set off for Cornwall; she looses her puppy fat and by the time she reaches the grand old age of eighteen is a slim and willowy young woman. She marries John Dudley a village lad, and they have two girls in rapid fire.

John is called up for army training and service in 1917, and goes into the trenches at Zonnebeke in Flanders to resist the German offensives in the spring of 1918. A shell lands 'plop' like a giant autumn acorn almost between his feet, and he is blown to chops.

Alice is a serene and fine looking woman in her forties when in the second war she meets a Canadian Soldier looking for the open arms of a grateful woman. He is only half her age, and fails of course to inform her that he has a fiancée called Anne; a Canadian girl serving in the catering corps with the RAF down in Cornwall.

Later Darren gets posted to North Africa.

Jake Jones: it almost hurts one's heart to speak his name; so far to go in so few years; and is this pain then just of loss.

A foreshortened life… a foreshortened leg with its cruelly poisoned stump… from warm wet kisses of admiring inspiring girls the day he joined the army, but at what cost… 'he should have died hereafter'.

Disraeli: now there's a name to conjure with, and he shall not grow old as in the real world Bobs and Baskin grow old.

Michael Sparks: enjoys long happy years… and three more kids, twin boys and another girl; but their big sister rules the roost.

Dee O'Mahony: yes that's her name, she started life in the lovely town of Sligo right beside that big rushing river that runs through between all the pink and green and blue houses; she was the wife of Mike in life but not on paper... they were not actually married.

Her Irish blood must give her that wayward romantic streak... at fifty-three she goes home to Sligo for a visit without Mike, except she takes Annie's oldest daughter Laura with her.

Veronica Oldham (Ronnie): becomes a good friend to Dee O'Mahony, and Annie too; the three even take a trip to Paris together later on.

Ken Oldham: loves his life and his routines... a bit too much perhaps. He and Ronnie go their separate ways a while after the Blackjack thing, though not because! But he is always favourite uncle when a year or so on Ronnie mysteriously gives birth to a little girl she calls Roseanne.

Annabel Coleen Sparks (Annie): well, what can you say! There was little question she would thrive.

A young woman with an ear for words, a zest for life, and a canny instinct that seeks out peoples' thoughts.

When she reaches the sixth form she gets good grades in her exams at school, and on to get a good degree in journalism. Annie starts work with a local paper then goes freelance... until her first novel is published!

Yes I nearly forgot someone... Bobcat-cat the cat: he doesn't get a good degree at university, or go on to do anything very startling, he just carries on being a cat; well it's the only thing he's good at.

In his eighteenth year his ninth life peters out... so does

that mean he had one life for every two years? Of course not, he got through the first eight of them in the eight weeks he 'went walkabout'... but the ninth one lasted him pretty well.

Some words or thoughts that were not by the author

Any nightingales or yellow moons: Edgar Phillips 1921

Anytime that air gets sniffed or dreaming starts might be Siegfried Sassoon. Also 'and treetops dark against the stars grown pale etc.' or any form of 'crimson gloom' and 'She sniffs the morning air' is also SS

But 'snuffed' air is always Edmund Blunden

'Paris, where twice green the trees do salute the year': Edward Shanks

'And in his eyes, the cold stars etc.' and 'He sat in his wheeled chair etc.' and 'Now he will never feel how slim girls waists are etc.' or 'a bitter cud etc.': Wilfred Owen

'When evening spreads its sail across the sky': T S Eliot I think

'Spring brings back blue days and fair': Alan Seeger

'He should have died hereafter', Macbeth; though it would be she rather than 'he': Will Shakespeare.

'Shoogaluubadooba', it was what my granddad Derwent invented as a quasi swear word he could use in front of the children (my mum etc) if he hit his thumb with a hammer.

Glossary of terms recurring in this book

Blighty: a name from two world wars, or perhaps before, that soldiers gave to their homeland.

'Cat': a relatively small but highly persistent quadruped that you love too much... and who both makes and wrecks your life...

Detrain: an equally uncommon military word, meaning when you finish a train journey.

Entrain: a rather rarely used word these days, that means to embark on a train journey... a term as detrain, used mostly by the military.

Kudos: meaning to receive glory or admiration.

Rec: is short for recreation ground.

'Rece': from the word reconnaissance. In general usage more like 'to take a butchers'.

'Seg': a Postal workers word, meaning to segregate sizes and type of mail.

Zenith: when the sun is at its highest point in the sky each day.

...See you on another journey, Mark

Printed in Great Britain
by Amazon